"What did you want to talk about?" Vayle asked, a little hesitantly, perhaps sensing the change in the air. The change in her very destiny.

"I had intended to talk about a great many things. But I've come to accept that while what has come before matters, it isn't as vital as what comes next."

A pulse leapt in her throat. Nelios curled his hand over his ankle when a different need struck. The need to reacquaint himself with the silky skin overlaying that pulse.

He accepted that all these months later, a peculiar kind of longing remained. That perhaps he'd left that Buenos Aires bedroom too quickly.

"And what exactly is that?"

He looked from mother to child and back again, that primitive claiming that defied civility and reason taking full, complete control of him.

"That I want my son. And I will have him. And because you will put up all sorts of a fight—which I will win, by the way—the culmination of it all will be that you will marry me. As soon as possible."

Maya Blake's hopes of becoming a writer were born when she picked up her first romance at thirteen. Little did she know her dream would come true! Does she still pinch herself every now and then to make sure it's not a dream? Yes, she does! Feel free to pinch her, too, via X, Facebook or Goodreads! Happy reading!

Books by Maya Blake

Harlequin Presents

The Greek's Forgotten Marriage
Pregnant and Stolen by the Tycoon
Snowbound with the Irresistible Sicilian
Enemy's Game of Revenge

Diamonds of the Rich and Famous

Accidentally Wearing the Argentinian's Ring

A Diamond in the Rough

Greek Pregnancy Clause

Royals of Cartana

Crowned for His Son
Out of Office Nights
Snowbound and Royally Forbidden

Visit the Author Profile page
at Harlequin.com for more titles.

KEEPING A GREEK SECRET

MAYA BLAKE

PRESENTS

If you purchased this book without a cover you should be aware that this book is stolen property. It was reported as "unsold and destroyed" to the publisher, and neither the author nor the publisher has received any payment for this "stripped book."

Recycling programs for this product may not exist in your area.

ISBN-13: 978-1-335-21357-0

Keeping a Greek Secret

Copyright © 2026 by Maya Blake

All rights reserved. No part of this book may be used or reproduced in any manner whatsoever without written permission.

Without limiting the exclusive rights of any author, contributor or the publisher of this publication, any unauthorized use of this publication to train generative artificial intelligence (AI) technologies is expressly prohibited. Harlequin also exercises their rights under Article 4(3) of the Digital Single Market Directive 2019/790 and expressly reserves this publication from the text and data mining exception.

This is a work of fiction. Names, characters, places and incidents are either the product of the author's imagination or are used fictitiously. Any resemblance to actual persons, living or dead, businesses, companies, events or locales is entirely coincidental.

For questions and comments about the quality of this book, please contact us at CustomerService@Harlequin.com.

TM and ® are trademarks of Harlequin Enterprises ULC.

Harlequin Enterprises ULC
22 Adelaide St. West, 41st Floor
Toronto, Ontario M5H 4E3, Canada
www.Harlequin.com

HarperCollins Publishers
Macken House, 39/40 Mayor Street Upper,
Dublin 1, D01 C9W8, Ireland
www.HarperCollins.com

Printed in Lithuania

KEEPING A GREEK SECRET

CHAPTER ONE

Prologos. Parados. Epeisodion. Stasimon. Exodus.

The stages of a Greek tragedy according to the great Aristotle. Nelios Petralis boarded his private jet at London's City Airport half-hoping he was at the denouement: exodus.

The finale of a decades-long plot was close but not quite close enough. He hadn't asked for his life to turn out this way. He'd been plunged into a harrowing drama by those who should've made better choices. But, while he hadn't started it, by God he intended to finish it on *his* terms.

Cradling his favourite tipple—aged whiskey that cost more than the average man's monthly salary—he stared over the crystal glass at his right-hand man, Andreas Barbieri. He and Andreas had found each other at possibly the worst moment of their lives: cornered in a filthy alley with half a dozen bullies twice their size baying for their blood, all because they'd stolen a loaf of bread 'on their patch'. They hadn't perished that day, obviously, but they'd come far too close.

Nelios eyed Andreas's Brioni suit, Savile Row tie and sleek Ulysse Nardin watch with a heartening sense of satisfaction. The outer trappings of success clawed out of the gutter, literally and figuratively. He didn't ask the question bristling on his tongue—whether Andreas had ever imagined they would be here today—because he didn't crave a trip down memory lane.

The three-hour meeting he'd just come from, one peppered with hoarsely voiced anguish and crocodile tears mingled with the stench of fear—from his opponents, never him—had been enough revisiting of his history for one day. His only regret was that another of those opponents had slipped his net through death some years ago—and, infuriatingly, remembering that fact still sent a lance of rage-tinged, wholly undeserving grief and regret through him, but that couldn't be changed.

He took another sip, savouring the exquisite taste, just as Andreas looked up.

'The meeting with the architects will start as soon as we take off. Would you like to go over the blueprints beforehand?' he asked with a trace of the Sicilian accent he'd never lost, despite having been dumped in Athens decades ago, just like Nelios.

'Not just yet,' he murmured. The low, dark throb in his voice echoed the rumbling within him. The rumbling he had every intention of ignoring because it always went away. Whiskey and a little distance always put him back on an even keel. Although…this *stasimon* might take a little longer.

He hadn't quite accounted for the little extra drama this afternoon in the form of the young woman full of fiery temper and righteous indignation. Definitely hadn't expected the heat stirring through him when in the boardroom she'd defiantly hurled her, 'I'll make sure you regret this if it's the last thing I do!'

'How is the other matter unfolding?' he asked now, with an extra-punchy layer of anticipation he didn't quite care for, and yet couldn't seem to discard. 'Is she on her way?'

Eyes so dark they looked black, and vicious in some lights, glinted at him as Andreas's brow quirked. 'As predicted. Our spies came through. She is walking through the terminal as we speak. Guess she intends on carrying through with her threat.'

Neither of them even glanced out of the window at the VIP terminal where more drama was unfolding. Andreas shook his head. 'It's shocking how very little money it takes for nos to turn into yeses when your name is dropped.'

Nelios smiled wryly. 'It's not just my name—yours too.' Although he knew his was weighty enough to swing things his way when required. 'And economies everywhere are in the toilet. People do what they must to get by with a little incentive.' *Like we had to.*

A sage nod from Andreas concurred that they'd both been there and done that, right before his phone pinged with an incoming text. His friend's satisfied grunt said everything Nelios needed to know. He hadn't set the trap, but he'd known about it almost the second it'd been created. And he intended to make full use of it.

He drained his glass as Andreas rose and headed for the front of the plane. In low tones, he informed the pilot and crew that they were ready for take-off—complete with their cheeky little stowaway. They'd been informed, on Nelios's orders, not to raise the alarm or do anything about it.

For the better part of two decades—ever since he'd ditched the name given to him at birth by undeserving parents who'd turned out to be faithless and cruel, and dragged himself and his new name from the gutters of Athens—he'd planned every corner of his life with lethal precision.

The woman who was sneaking her way onto his private jet with the sole purpose of somehow disrupting his plans to take over her hotel—an all but done deal with very small fry indeed—shouldn't have mattered this much, yet somehow…

He shifted in his seat, wondering just why she mattered to him. Was it because she was now connected to those who'd wronged him all those years ago? Because those scant minutes when she'd stood up to him in their meeting earlier replayed in his head with a vividness he couldn't dismiss? Because her earnest desperation and flaming determination had struck a chord with him?

Whatever. He hated unsolved puzzles. That was all she was, he assured himself. And, by placing herself within his orbit, he could be done with this silly conundrum by the time he stopped to refuel. And, hell, maybe he could learn a thing or two about his enemies while he was at it.

A full hour later, long after his plane had taken off and levelled out over the clouds of the Atlantic, and his meeting with his architects had been satisfactorily concluded, Nelios rose from his club chair.

Andreas's teeth bared as they did whenever he scented a conquest. Sometimes it was hard to believe anyone on earth was more bloodthirsty than Nelios, but here he was, witnessing the stark truth on his friend's face. 'Happy hunting.'

Nelios grunted. 'The hunt was over even before it began, my friend. The real question is, what to do with my unwanted prey?'

His friend's low laughter echoed in his ears as Nelios strode to the back of the plane, entered his bedroom, stretched out on his bed…

And waited.

She'd done it.

Dear God.

Vayle Lancaster couldn't stop the shivers from unravelling through her, despite the adrenaline having fled her system hours ago. She was grateful for the tight closet bracing her back and knees otherwise she would've collapsed into a pathetic heap long ago.

From the glow of her phone screen she watched the countdown: another five long hours of being stuck in this closet. Then she could enact the next part of her plan. With any luck, she could be back home by the end of the day tomorrow.

Argentina was still hours away, though. No way would she make it all the way there hiding in Nelios Petralis's wardrobe. Especially when the scent swirling around in here made her even dizzier.

God, how did he smell so good?

By being filthy rich and having parfumiers and other rich people's accessories at his fingertips, that's how.

She shook her head. True but not entirely. She'd noticed, with much annoyance and alarm while caught in that one-way verbal spat—because Nelios Petralis hadn't lifted even an eyebrow when she'd let loose the volley of anger at his treatment of them—that the other guy, his right-hand man, smelled good too. But Vayle hadn't fixated on his scent the way she had on Petralis's.

Fixated? A rather strong word. But no other word accurately described how she couldn't get it out of her senses. How she wanted to keep breathing it in as if it was vital oxygen…

Enough. Concentrate!

She wrapped her arms around her knees. It was a good thing she was neither claustrophobic nor afraid of the dark. That she was used to contorting herself into tight spaces.

Distressing memories tried to crowd her brain but she shook her head free of them and glanced back at her phone. She wished for a split second she'd thought to pack her earbuds, before she snorted under her breath. This wasn't some jolly jaunt. Bopping to her favourite music wasn't an option when she needed to remain alert. To listen out for her chance with Nelios Petralis when he came into his bedroom.

Would he be angry or display that fathoms-deep icy indifference he'd basked in all through their meeting this afternoon? The meeting, she recalled with horror, that had devolved into tears from her surrogate mother and a shocking lack of decorum from Vayle herself—but who could blame her? Far from meeting with Nelios to come to an agreement about a possible business agreement regarding her hotel, as she'd thought, he'd informed her coldly that he was stealing her inheritance right from under her nose!

Vayle wasn't even sure which reaction she'd prefer. Both were terrifying. But, fortunately, not enough to dissuade her. She knew her subject matter inside and out. Knew like the back of her hand the hotel he was trying to annex. It bore her name, for heaven's sake. Just as she knew that what she had to offer was everything he'd refused to accommodate in this cruel hostile takeover he seemed bent on pursuing, despite her hotel being ludicrously below his radar.

Four hours, forty-five minutes, then she could state her case, calmly and concisely and hope he listened and didn't do anything drastic, like fling her out of his aeroplane from forty thousand feet into the frigid Atlantic.

Breathe, Vayle. Breathe.

Stowing away on his private jet had been a bonkers idea from the start but the potentially scary part—in which she'd imagined she would be caught before she boarded and thrown in jail—had gone surprisingly smoothly. Which didn't say a lot for aviation security, but she would lament that observation another day. The second, scarier part was still ahead of her so she needed to stay calm for a little bit longer.

She dropped her forehead onto her knees, practising the yoga breath-control she'd striven to master through turbulent years when the slightest misstep could set tempers flaring. Banishing her to the dark.

Thankfully, those years were behind her. She just needed to do this one last thing for Agnes Adamis—her 'surrogate mother'—the woman who'd opened her heart and arms to Vayle when she'd needed it most.

Bonkers or not, it was the very least she could do. Agnes could've returned to Greece after her husband Tolis's death, as she'd strongly hinted at doing, but she'd stayed with Vayle and helped her through her own complicated grief after she'd lost the father with whom she'd had a fraught relationship. Even Agnes's confession immediately after the meeting that Nelios's treatment of them was her fault—that their past history had led to this—hadn't dissuaded Vayle from pushing back against this billionaire's bullying tactics. Hell, it'd only spurred her on. She knew a thing or two about bullies—her father had been one, hiding behind illness to make everyone's life an absolute misery.

Whatever Nelios Petralis was hiding behind to treat Vayle and the woman she held dear like this—the woman who, shockingly, also happened to be his mother—she would hold him to account, if it was the last thing she did.

Purpose reasserted, she eyed the timer. Many more hours yet.

It wouldn't hurt to close her eyes, stay calm and just breathe. Breathe. Breathe...

She wasn't sure what woke her but the sound was far too close. Adrenaline roared through her system, making her jerk and... *Argh!*

'Oh...oh crap! Oh God!' The deadly cramp gripped her

hamstring like vicious teeth sinking into her flesh and had her crying out a second time.

She scrambled out of the wardrobe on her hands and one knee while desperately trying to straighten her other leg and flex her foot to ease the wildly spasming muscle. It didn't budge. Hell, it got worse...

'Ah, there you are. I was wondering how long you intended to nap.'

Vayle froze, her stunned gaze falling on a set of feet. *Bare masculine feet.* Dry mouthed, her eyes moved up, inch by inch to bare, thick hair-roughened calves...bare knees...

Oh my God.

She should've averted her gaze then, and stopped this comedy of errors dead in its tracks, but no. Her stupefied gaze kept climbing. *Climbing...*

The tiniest layer of tension punched out when, thankfully, her gaze met the edge of a pristine white towel. But that dissipated quickly as another savage spasm ripped through her leg. She dropped and rolled over at his feet, her hands scrambling to grip her muscle.

'What is wrong with you?' the dark, unfortunately familiar voice bit out.

She winced. 'Cramp. Help, please!' Vayle couldn't believe the tears that sprang to her eyes. She never, ever cried, no matter what. So what was this? Maybe she was more sleep-deprived than she'd thought.

No; going without sleep was another talent she could claim to possess. She'd always needed to keep one eye open in case George Lancaster—the vicious half-man, all monster, who'd biologically fathered her, and the man with a temperament trickier than mercury—had decided to torment her while she was asleep and unguarded. She'd learnt to withhold her tears and her protests, her silent defiance and lack of engagement eventually outlasting his sometimes hours-long rants.

She'd been through some of the worst emotional torture a human being could withstand without shedding a single tear, and yet here she was, crying over a cramp.

Teeth gritted, she dropped onto the plush carpet, noting that he hadn't moved a single muscle to help her. *Bastard.* Lying on her back, she lifted her leg and tried to massage the spasm out of her calf but the more she tried, the worse it seemed to get.

'Are you serious right now?' The words were muttered incredulously.

Her eyes opened, helplessly drawn back to him, and she was granted an even more disturbing sight.

Nelios Petralis's entire body, clad in just a towel. His wet, damp hair fell over his face as he glowered at her. His unshaven jaw clamped tight. And his far too sensual lips were thin with disapproval.

Even upside down he was beyond spectacular, virile in a way that left zero doubt as to his rampant maleness, his dominance at the top of the food chain.

She rolled onto her side, as if that would dissipate both his overwhelming presence and the tearing ache in her flesh. Neither happened. Another cry tore past her guard and Vayle wanted to disappear. To find the strength to get up and fling herself out of the nearest opening.

Because this was mortifying... And agonising. And possibly her own fault for not hydrating enough. But she'd been too nervous to eat, never mind drink, once she'd made up her mind about her contingency plan for tackling Nelios Petralis.

'I'll do whatever I can to get his attention,' she'd said to Agnes. 'Even stow away on his plane if I must. Actually, that might be the only option. He's building his latest hotel in Buenos Aires and he's flying there tonight. I'll have several hours of his undivided attention to make him see sense.'

Agnes's tear-filled argument against Vayle's wild plan had nearly dissuaded her. But the other woman's clear anguish when she'd insisted that she deserved everything Nelios Petralis—her own son—was doing to her had filled Vayle with a deeper purpose. Intensely hot billionaire, with a body carved like the best of Greek gods or not, Vayle would not let him get away with this.

So here she was, sprawled on her back, contemplating her choices and writhing in agony while... Her breath punched out of her when a strong pair of hands gripped her flailing leg.

'Stay still.' The instruction was cold and terse, the very opposite of the warmth that bracketed her when he planted her bare foot against his abs. She froze, less in line with his command and more in reaction to the sensation of the searing skin-to-skin contact. Captive, she watched as, with two fingers, he dug into her calf muscle, right at the epicentre of her agony. Vayle gasped as her muscles spasmed in opposition...for several seconds...then gave way beneath the pressure. Her moan of relief was unguarded, bouncing above the sound of the humming aeroplane engines to fill the room.

The muscles beneath her foot clenched and unclenched, his dark gaze narrowing on her face as he continued to tend to her. She couldn't help herself. Another moan threatened as relief poured through her, her agony subsiding. But with the lessening of one trauma came the resurgence of what she faced. Why she was here.

Nelios's deadly gaze told her that reality would come

with a great reckoning. She attempted to remove her foot from his skin, but one hand dropped over the top of her foot, keeping it flush against him.

'It's a little too late for retreat now, Miss Lancaster.'

Several things fell into place then. His comment about her taking a nap when she'd tumbled out of his wardrobe. His lack of surprise.

He'd known she was here all along.

She tried once more to free herself. Displeasure flashed across his face as he held her still. 'Your cramp hasn't subsided. And, as entertaining as it is to watch you flop about on my floor, I have better things to do. Stay still,' he repeated, 'And let me finish.'

Dear God. The rumble of his voice... The power behind it... The towering magnificence of him... He was indeed a Greek god come to life, complete with all the bells and whistles of furious thunder and incandescent lightning. She was shocked she hadn't been incinerated beneath the force of his wrath.

And yes, he was angry. It was there in the stiff shoulders and clenched jaw. Or...was it something else? Because beneath the arctic gaze there was something mesmeric, shimmering with heat, with awareness. Striations of white-hot heat. Of attraction...?

No. Absolutely not.

Pain, and then the beginnings of relief from it, was addling her brain. She dragged her gaze over his shoulder, pinning it to the ceiling as she tried to ignore everything but the countdown to tackling her task. To letting him know unequivocally what she thought of him and his bullying tactics. Then, maybe, to striking some kind of deal. Because she couldn't lose.

'That's how you're going to play it?' he mused dryly.

'Pretend I don't exist? That's going to make it difficult for you to achieve your ultimate goals, is it not?'

Her gaze darted to him. 'What do you know about my goals?' she asked hesitantly, feeling him out.

A muscle twitched in his cheek. 'I'm assuming you didn't stow away on my plane for the sole purpose of taking a nap in my wardrobe and inconveniencing me and my driving need for a shower for over two hours?'

The apology on the tip of her tongue dried when she realised he was mocking her. Had he truly needed to shower hours ago, he would've taken one. He'd showered exactly when he'd needed to, all the while being aware she was hiding amongst his clothes.

A flush built in her face but Vayle refused to look away. 'If you knew I was in here, then why…?'

'Why did I not do something about it? Where would the fun have been in that?'

She flinched and stifled another gasp when his thumb dug in deeper and slowly worked its way to the top of her Achilles tendon. Goodness, he might be a monster, but he was an expert at unknotting muscles. Why that thought suffused her with several waves of heat, she absolutely refused to contemplate as she attempted to remove herself from his grip again. And failed…again. But the movement dislodged the object in her pocket.

His gaze trailed to the right. She followed it to her phone screen: the timer displayed in bright red. 'And what is that clock counting down to? You locating your courage?' he taunted. 'Or rousing yourself from your beauty sleep?'

Irritation zipped through her. 'Neither. It's for when we took off again, after refuelling.'

'I see. At which point you'd believe I would be unwilling

to turn back the plane or take steps to eject you entirely?' he enquired silkily.

Vayle squirmed beneath the incisiveness of his gaze. She knew her nerves and lack of a decent poker face gave her away but, she told herself, since that was exactly what she'd hoped, why hide from it? 'Yes.'

'Hmm.' It was very perturbing that this man was so livid with her, yet he continued to tend to her as if he had all the time in the world. As if she were a person in need he cared about.

Which was a vicious lie. Kindness and consideration were the last things he was capable of. For the better part of a year she'd watched him decimate the hotel she co-managed with Agnes, stealing contracts and clients right from under their noses and not even bothering to disguise what he was doing. He was systematically driving them out of business so he could scoop up what remained.

So this had to be a trick. An apex predator toying with his prey. His hands wreaked magic on her body while those eyes continued to flash hot and cold, keeping her guessing as to his true emotions.

With more power than she'd thought herself capable of, considering her insides veritably quivered with the nerves eating her alive, she yanked her foot from his hold.

This time she succeeded. Or he let her go. She scrambled back until her spine hit the side of the enormous bed. And he watched her with sizzling focus as she tried to compose herself, flex her foot and with relief note that the throb had substantially decreased. She curbed the urge to check the hair she could feel unravelling from its neat knot, or the grey pencil-skirt and jacket that she'd cobbled together to pass muster as one of his flight attendants. Glad when she managed both, she darted a glance at him and saw his folded-arms stance, the eyebrow raised in rigid expectation.

She licked her lips. 'You know why I'm here.'

His gaze slowly raked over her, the tiniest escalation in his breathing telling her he wasn't as supremely cool as he projected. 'Do I? Or should the more pertinent question be, why the hell should I care?' Before she could launch into the spiel she'd practised repeatedly since their meeting, he continued. 'You're adequately intelligent enough to know you've broken several laws. Shouldn't you concern yourself with navigating that dilemma before anything else?'

She opened her mouth to speak, then a cold shiver washed over her. 'So you knew I was onboard, and you deliberately let me hide in here just so you could get me into trouble? Is that your idea of fun?'

His head tilted. 'Let me get this straight. Are you attempting to make me somehow responsible for your crimes?' he mused, then every hint of amusement evaporated. 'I shouldn't be surprised, considering who reared you, and yet...' The hard edge embedded in his voice abruptly cut off, leaving her short of breath.

Because in those last words she'd witnessed a complex mine of emotions, every single one of them containing ferocious charges set to detonate at the smallest friction.

Who reared you...

Whether he was referring to George Lancaster, or Agnes and her late husband Tolis, she wasn't sure. Both Tolis and her father had died within weeks of each other, eighteen months ago, the former from a stroke and the latter after a short and violent illness that had screeched in like an evil wind and taken him with it. It was a shockingly apt metaphor for how he'd lived his life and the anguish he'd left behind. And, while Tolis hadn't been as affable as his wife, Vayle was in the dark as to why his son was so bitter.

But acrimonious family history wasn't why she was here. She was here to save her inheritance, regardless of the despair shrouding it. Or maybe it was *because* of the despair that she fought so hard. Because all these years of suffering surely would have been for nothing if she couldn't turn Vayle Hotel into a happy and welcoming place.

'We're getting off on the wrong foot,' she started, only to halt when he barked out arid laughter.

'No, Miss Lancaster. You and I will not be getting off anywhere—ever.' The words hovered, dark, ominous and… curiously electrifying, before he added, 'We will be touching down on Ascension in the next hour. You will be handed over to the authorities with a full account of how you lied your way through the airport by pretending to be a member of my crew to gain access to my jet, then hid away with the intent of…doing me harm? Attempted poisoning, suffocation or strangulation? Which is more salacious, do you think?'

Her mouth gaped as her mind spun. 'I was right, wasn't I? You…knew and you let it happen.'

'I knew,' he confirmed with zero inflection, as if he were confirming a menu selection. 'Every step of the way.' He shrugged. 'I may have even eased your way just to see if you'd go through with it. Your commitment in the face of possible arrest was quite…something.' Again his eyes seemed to sizzle over her, his brows pinching faintly before he shook his head, as if freeing himself from a thrall.

She swallowed, ignoring her own elevated temperature. *Now* she knew why it'd seemed so easy to saunter past all the checkpoints that should've been more rigorous. He'd been watching, the ultimate puppet master as she'd strung herself up. She experienced a futile nanosecond of unadulterated fury with him before she wised up.

This was no one's fault but hers. Even if she actively detested his *where's the fun in that?* she'd willingly stepped into this trap. And, as she knew from years of torment at her father's hand, it was entirely up to her how she dealt with it. Curling herself into a ball and wailing was not an option.

Slowly she straightened her no longer spasming leg, flexing it again to test that it was indeed cramp-free before she manoeuvred onto her knees. Just before she rose to her feet, something hot and lethal flashed in his eyes, but it was gone far too quickly to decipher its origin or purpose. 'You said we have an hour before we land?'

He didn't answer, but his eyes narrowed that extra fraction, warning her that whatever she was about to demand wouldn't be well received.

She ploughed ahead because…she really had no choice. She hadn't done all this to back down now. 'That thing you said about the way I was reared…' Her heart lurched and she almost lost the power of speech when his eyes turned several degrees more arctic. 'You couldn't be more wrong. Because, while not my blood relatives, your mother, Agnes—and Tolis when he was alive—were more loving and generous to me than my own parent ever was. So, no, I wasn't *reared* like some wild and unruly farm animal, as you so insultingly implied, and…'

Vayle stuttered to a stop as the man before her turned into a statue. But, while his body froze, the complex mine of emotions cracked and fizzled through his eyes like the most devastating fireworks. The blood rushed from her head, making her stagger back one step, then another, until the back of her legs met the bed and she couldn't retreat further.

Still caught in the vortex of his eyes, she watched him

pivot to face the wardrobe that'd been her hiding place. And, with zero warning, Nelios Petralis dropped his towel.

She told herself her knees weakened because of the deadly currents flying through the air. And while that was very true—dear heaven, why had her words triggered such an intense reaction from him?—she didn't even equivocate about her body's searing response to being presented with the most visually magnificent man she'd ever seen. A man whose body belonged in the annals for mortal men and women to study those mile-wide shoulders and the muscles that moved beneath them; the olive-hued perfection of his skin; the tight glutes that formed his gloriously impressive ass; the tree-trunk legs that could down a lion with stupefying vigour.

This was a man who had zero compunction about being naked in front of her. Did he want to scandalise her, perhaps? No, Vayle concluded as her fists bunched in the high-thread-count sheets; she was almost certain that wasn't the case.

The simple truth was that her words had triggered something in Nelios Petralis. Something so primal, raw and lethal, he'd momentarily acted purely on autopilot.

CHAPTER TWO

You couldn't be more wrong.

A string of impassioned words meant to sway him. To alter his goals, perhaps view the chessboard from her angle.

Not blood relatives... Loving and generous...

Something thick, noxious and near-terrifying locked in his throat, roared in his ears and hazed his eyes. For a full minute he couldn't see, feel or hear anything but those words.

He'd never once in his life felt as if he could hyperventilate into unconsciousness, not even when he'd been cornered by thugs and terrified out of his mind as a weak, malnourished boy of thirteen. And yet, standing there, stark-naked with his towel at his feet, Nelios wagered that he might be as close to doing so as he'd ever been. Because every cell in his body was locked in bitterness and acute disbelief...

He couldn't be more right. Because he'd lived that torturous reality. He knew down to his very marrow how it felt to have his every last hope dashed, his world turn to ash just for the hell of it. No, not for the hell of it. For thirty pieces of silver; a loftier position in life. To elevate oneself regardless of how it affected others. Oh yes, in his case it had been all of the above for the two people who'd callously tossed him away. Sure they'd debated the toss for a handful of days but it'd been more a circling of wagons than opting for a different path—a path that didn't involve the ruthless abandonment of their only child.

He sensed her behind him, wondering if and why her words had turned him into a seething mass of ice at the side of a mountain, waiting for the smallest trigger to unleash the raging avalanche he could feel just beneath the surface.

He owed her neither his agita nor his explanation. But with every breath he took, those handful of words reverberated through him, demanding a response, an outlet.

This afternoon he'd seen the evidence of what she'd so passionately proclaimed. At first, he hadn't wanted to believe it. He'd thought his eyes were playing tricks on him. But then he'd caught the warm, fond smile Agnes Adamis had slanted her and had wondered whether she'd received the same from Tolis when he was alive.

He'd seen the wide, encouraging smile Vayle had returned and he'd marvelled at *how a monster could smile*. How the woman who'd given him life, then turned her back on him, could project *fondness*. He had indeed skated to the edge of that abyss he'd stared into many times in years gone by and wondered if *he* was problem. If he'd sinned so egregiously in a past life that he'd deserved to be punished in this one.

Then he'd reminded himself that even *he* smiled on occasion. Usually right before he crushed his enemies beneath his polished Italian leather shoes. Certainly he and Andreas had smiled over the years as they'd bested every single person who'd wronged them. And, with each billion they'd added to their bank account, he'd *marvelled* and *smiled* through being screamed at and being cursed and cajoled for mercy, usually by the very people who were the epitome of mercilessness.

So, yes, he had put that smile between Agnes and Vayle out of his mind. But now, to hear Vayle putting her spin on it, urging him to believe it was for other reasons besides being utterly monstrous... The sheer gall of that was the abomination, not him.

'Say something.' Her husky entreaty chiselled the tiniest crack in the dense ice.

His emotions, locked down tightly and buried beneath the filthy alleys somewhere back in Athens, groaned beneath the weight of it. Fingers convulsed around the forgotten scrap of fabric he'd grabbed, he turned back round.

Her eyes, wide and luminous with a flurry of emotions, frantically searched his face. Then, her cheeks growing pinker by the second, those eyes dropped down his naked body to his chest, his abs, his groin...

And, to add absolute insult to injury, there in the cabin that she'd invaded with her unwanted presence, her loathsome views and unfounded judgements, Nelios felt his traitorous body react to her nonplussed, wide-eyed scrutiny. He felt the stirrings that had begun in the conference room this afternoon, and had risen to a low simmer as he'd waited for her to sneak onto his plane, then spark into an unconscionable blaze, stunning the hell out of him.

A growl built in his throat as he shook out the boxers he clutched and, daring her with his eyes to utter one word at his blatant erection, he yanked on his underwear.

Her cheeks puffed with the strength of her audible exhale as he once again pivoted to drag a pair of chinos and a T-shirt from his wardrobe.

Finally dressed, after what felt like hours after he'd first exited his bathroom, Nelios faced her once more.

Say something, she'd said. He approached, arms folded across his chest, his eyes pinned on her so there would be no mistaking his words.

'You want me to say something? I know exactly who she is, what kind of man my father was before he died—and, yes, I *will* speak ill of the dead. I know the evil they're capable of. You may have been fooled into putting on those rose-tinted glasses you're proudly wearing but know this: that woman will throw you away like unwanted garbage the second something better comes along.'

His mouth twisted and he chuckled past the constriction in his throat. 'What am I talking about? She already has! She's thrown you at me, at my mercy, without a second thought to what I would do to you when I discovered your intentions.'

'No…no she hasn't. She didn't. Coming here was—'

'Of your own free will? Or were you manipulated? Perhaps even cajoled with a well-timed tear or two? An entreaty that you were a last hope and therefore needed to do the right thing?'

He watched her pale, her expression spout suspicion right before she vehemently shook her head. 'No. If you'd just let me speak, I'd tell you it's not like that. This was my idea and mine alone. In case you haven't noticed, mine is the name on the hotel. I have a horse in this race too. As for Agnes, she's kind and decent, no matter how much you want to think otherwise. Look, I don't know what happened between you and your mother, but—'

Another growl rose and her head snapped up, her apprehension gone.

'You won't trick me into denying what I know to be true. Besides, how would you know?' she challenged. 'Your own parents rarely mentioned you in all the years I've known them. And you haven't been interested in them in return. You weren't even at Tolis's funeral. And yet, in the past year, you've been intent on tearing up our lives from the comfort of your plane, or your mansion or wherever monsters like you ooze from. So where's your proof that you know them at all?'

He stalked towards her, aware his teeth were bared. That years of locked emotions strained to explode from him. He wasn't at all surprised when she shrank back onto her elbows, her breathing choppy as he stopped mere feet from her. Yes, he was monstrous. But then wasn't he a product of monsters?

His arms dropped to his sides, his fists curling. 'Where is my evidence? Open your eyes. Take a good look, Miss Lancaster. I was theirs too, once. But, unlike you, I was the child Apostolis and Agnes Adamis actually conceived. The son they reared from birth until I was twelve years old. The child they tolerated like a low-priority pet. Until a shiny new prospect was offered to them. And then, with neither kindness nor consideration, they threw me away. So, yes.' His fist slammed his chest in an act far too emotionally reminiscent of the *stasimon* he wished to be done with, but no matter. 'I am living, breathing proof of exactly what I'm talking about.'

From some dim corner of her brain Vayle examined the veracity of his words. Debated whether he was accomplished enough to spout such vicious lies with a straight, albeit breathtaking face. Because they *were* lies; they had to be. And yet the majority of her reasoning took in the complexities of elevated breathing and the bleak rage in those eyes fixed so ferociously on hers. Took in the stern brackets around his thinned lips and the jagged roughness of his voice that blared the evidence that he'd been pushed into confessing. Pushed to the edge—by her.

Vayle knew she would have to come up with something unassailable to refute what her senses screamed at her was the truth. A *horrifying* truth.

'I know you're their son.' Those brown eyes, which were a shade darker than Agnes's, and the male version of her mouth made it irrefutable. And she supposed his jet-black hair matched Tolis's, although his father's had turned more grey than black in the few years before his death. 'Even though your surnames are different. And... I've known them for nearly two decades. Agnes had told me a tiny bit about you, but only that she'd lost you. I thought you were...'

She pursed her lips, not wanting to repeat or recall Agnes's anguish when she'd spoken about her son. For years Vayle had believed 'lost' meant 'died', until she'd recently learned differently. 'There has to be a better explanation for what happened than they threw you away.'

She couldn't wrap her mind around what he was saying about the couple who'd arrived to helm her father's flagship hotel after the banks and doctors had declared George Lancaster unfit to keep managing his own affairs.

Over the years they'd become like parents to Vayle, protecting her from her father's many torments until his death, while co-managing the hotel with her after she'd finished university, and mentoring her to take over her inheritance one day.

While Tolis had had his moments of obstinacy and mild misogyny, he'd been miles better than her own father. Definitely not the parent Nelios had described.

Nelios took a step back, his emotions rapidly wrestled

under control so he could stare down at her with something strongly resembling pity.

'Is that the only straw in your sinking raft, Miss Lancaster?' he mocked. 'I changed my name at the first opportunity because I couldn't abide the stench of it a second longer. Those people abandoned me and I renounced them legally on what was one of the best days of my life.' The thick vein of satisfaction, victory and loathing in his voice said he was reliving the memory with much relish.

She shuddered, still unable to reconcile the two realities. One *had* to be a distortion.

'You keep saying they threw you away, abandoned you. How...how is that even possible?'

His eyes narrowed. 'What were you told?'

She licked her lips, her pulse jumping when he followed the movement. Scrambling, she tried to recall what Agnes had told her about the son she found painful to talk about. 'Tolis, your father, rarely talked—' She stopped when he snarled under his breath. 'Agnes said they left you in Greece so you could continue your education. But that something happened, and they lost track of you...'

His teeth set harshly, his nostrils flaring for a moment before he turned away. She thought he would ignore her but surprisingly he spoke.

'Of course they would couch it in such vague terms.' He shook his head, his voice gravel-rough as he continued, 'I came home from school on a normal day to find someone my father claimed had been sent by a friend of his in our home. A friend who happened to run a foster-care agency. I was told I had to be placed with this stranger for a while, while my parents pursued a rosy future for us in England. What she didn't know was that even if we were destitute, I would have been prepared to live with them on the streets instead of being left behind.'

He stopped, clenched his jaw and exhaled. 'As I said, I knew they were lying. We weren't rich but we certainly weren't destitute. And they'd forgotten how thin the walls in our house were—that or they didn't care. I overheard them discussing it the night before but hadn't fully understood what I'd heard, until the foster carer arrived. It was my father's idea. My mother put up a token fight but she didn't hold out for long.'

His mouth twisted. 'And, yes, I said so to the carer. Gave her the real reason my parents were throwing me away. It was so they could make a better life for themselves in England, unencumbered by a child. She immediately marked me down as a troublemaker who liked to spin tales about his parents who were doing the right thing by seeking a better future for them and their child. The carer took their side, of course. Smiled approvingly as Tolis looked into my eyes and outright lied that they would be back in a year, when I'd heard them committing to at least three years in their new job the night before.'

His head snapped towards Vayle when she gasped.

His smile was a caricature of blinding white teeth. 'Oh yes, I know that means something to you. I know you recognise the stipulations regarding your father's guardianship. That the banks wanted whoever took over management of the hotel to be given a minimum three-year contract to ensure a stable tenure. And, yes, I know your father's extremely lucrative offer is what lured my parents. An offer which included the small but significant clause that whoever took the position should be *without encumbrances*. An offer they accepted.'

His body followed his head and he faced her once

more, a towering pillar of icy control. 'So, given the circumstances described to you, do you not think I was well within my rights to denounce them as they once denounced me?' His question was a silky blade slicing through her jumbled senses.

Her fingers twisted in her lap. 'But Agnes said she tried to keep in contact with you. She never forgot about you. That something must have gone wrong. Have you tried speaking to your mother about what happened, instead of causing all this destruction? Because there's likely a good reason for it…that they… There has to be.'

His frozen face turned grimmer. 'Does there? Why? Because it would suit your rosy outlook? Your fairy-tale imagination where you think you've been rescued from a fate worse than death, only to discover your fairy godparents were the real monsters all along?'

Something clogged in her throat. Something like horror… A sob… She swallowed it down and shook her head. 'I know nothing I say can…will…change your mind. But the truth is, I know what I know.'

His teeth bared again. 'Good. Keep believing what you wish to believe. If you're saving me all the melodrama by admitting you can't change my mind then we're done here, feel free to return to the wardrobe until we land, if you prefer, but I won't save you from another cramping episode, so bear that in mind.'

Vayle jumped up when he strode to the door. 'Hold on. I never said I wasn't willing to… I still need to talk to you about my hotel.'

He slanted her a mocking glance. 'You mean *my* hotel, seeing as you have no choice but to accept my offer? The simple answer is nothing. You've had a wasted journey and may well have an upcoming stint in jail to look forward to. Congratulations.' He pulled the door open and walked out.

Knowing she would have to follow him, and show herself to his crew, made her cringe and seriously consider taking his offer to dive back into his wardrobe. It took a monumental effort to lock her knees and reheat courage gone cold at his devastating revelations. Revelations she would need to unpack later because right now she simply could not reconcile the two realities. There *was* a missing link somewhere. Until then, though...

She staggered one step forward and, realising she'd lost her shoes somewhere in her mad, cramping tumble, glanced at the wardrobe. But Vayle knew the second she approached it she would take the cowardly option and dive back in. Return to yet another dark cupboard, but this time of her own volition.

So, feet bare and courage woefully tepid, she hurried after Nelios Petralis.

She found him in the jet's dining room—after several wrong turns and encounters with sharply dressed crew whose lack of surprise at an additional passenger's appearance proved they'd known of her presence all along. And that, in sharp contrast to their flawless attire, her poor imitation must have made her stick out like a sore thumb all through her doomed escapade.

She hovered in the doorway and watched Nelios and the other man with whom he'd attended the meeting this afternoon converse in low tones while devouring sumptuous-looking steaks. She knew that they were both actively ignoring her, and a spark of ire warmed up her courage. But, before she could speak, her stomach took charge, growling fiercely enough to stop them mid-conversation.

Dear God, could this get any worse?

Apparently it could. Because the conversation stopped once her belly finished its demanding aria. Nelios turned his imperious head, eyes scouring her as if she was the trash he had just informed her he'd been treated as by his parents. Trash *he* intended to throw away the second they landed.

So do something. Don't just stand there.

'Mr Petralis,' she started, only to stop when he held up an imperious hand then lowered it to drum on the table, his stare penetrating.

'I cannot think or eat to the unsavoury accompaniment of your stomach's soundtrack.' He yanked out the chair next to him. 'Sit down,' he snapped.

Annoyingly, since she had no leg to stand on, Vayle sat. A button was pressed. An attendant appeared. Lavish choices were offered. Within minutes a large prime steak, salad and the prettiest potatoes she'd ever seen on a plate was set before her. And, because she'd been programmed to never look gift horses in the mouth, and despite her face flaming when another discordant melody surged from her middle, she picked up her cutlery and ate.

She was aware they were both watching. Aware that, after a full minute, the other man murmured something in Greek to Nelios, reigniting their conversation. Which dragged a rake of irritation across her senses, ruffling them until she couldn't stay quiet.

'You know it's impolite to conduct a conversation when one party doesn't speak the language, don't you?'

Derisive brown eyes turned on her. 'By all means, tutor us in the correct etiquette of conversation while you breathe my air and eat my food, Miss Stowaway,' Nelios drawled.

The other man smirked. Vayle attempted a glare that bounced off his wide shoulders.

Let it go. Let it go. 'I'm just saying…'

'Here's a word of advice: know when to quit,' the man said, cutting a square of steak and chewing it.

Her gaze moved to Nelios and she saw a flash of something close to irritation in his eyes before he too resumed eating. Silence reigned, self-consciousness aggravating her already ragged senses.

She was setting down her cutlery when an attendant approached. 'We'll be landing to refuel in ten minutes, Mr Petralis.' The man, who looked more like a bodyguard than an attendant, darted a glance at Vayle before returning to his boss. 'The pilot wants to know whether you still want the authorities on standby as you previously requested?'

Without glancing at her, Nelios nodded, picked up his wine glass and drained it. 'Tell him nothing has changed. I want Miss Lancaster off my plane and handed over as soon as—'

'No, wait. Please don't. Look, I'll… I'll do anything!'

'Rookie mistake,' Andreas muttered under his breath five minutes after Vayle Lancaster had blurted that unexpected response, and he and Nelios had left her in the dining room without replying. 'I'm not sure whether I pity her or am amused by her. Either way, you're better off cutting her loose asap. I'll go grab the security. She'll be someone else's problem within the hour, my friend.' He walked away.

Outside, the flurry of activity rumbled on, including the squad car and two policemen waiting patiently to board with Nelios's permission.

He rolled his shoulders with a combination of irritation at his friend and the knowledge that he needed to heed Andreas's warning and cut her loose. He didn't need this drama. Didn't need the flare of heat across his skin whenever he looked at her face, at her mouth, heard the breathless quality of her speech or observed the way her damn eyelashes fluttered when she was agitated. He didn't need to remember how firm and supple her body had felt beneath his touch.

His latest creation, the Nelios XV hotel, was in the final stages of construction in Argentina and needed every ounce of his attention. It would be the milestone to mark the many he'd accrued over the years, and it was his first foray into South America, a place he'd fallen in love with.

A place where he'd also witnessed the kind of hardship that ravaged his soul. Which was why, alongside his hotel construction, he was also building special housing for desperate children, as he and Andreas had once been. Both projects were ambitious, with varying challenges, the kind he fully relished. But also the kind that needed his full attention. So why the hell did he hear her *I'll do anything* plea on repeat in his head?

He'd already let himself down in that bedroom by revealing truths he'd excised from his life. Yes, her words and blind belief in his parents had riled him like nothing else had for a very long time. He'd barely managed to snap that, contrary to her belief, he had attended his father's funeral. He had stood beneath a tree thirty feet away and watched the man who'd discarded him get put in the ground. Then he'd waited until everyone had departed, and he had stood over his grave—bitter, bewildered, angry and, much to his deep chagrin, a little lost.

Maybe it was that last sensation that had triggered this end game, the need for answers before time cruelly stole them from him.

Whatever.

And, yes, he'd concluded the quicker he ripped those

rose-tinted glasses off Vayle's face, the better for them all, because he wanted her to know exactly who Agnes Adamis truly was. Who Tolis had been. Wanted there to be no crumb of compassion left for them by the time he was done.

If Vayle cared enough to take the trouble, verification would only take her hours, days at most. Nelios had never bothered to hide his past. Hell, his first business venture had been one street away from that alley in which he'd nearly lost his life after he'd run away from the final foster home he'd been placed in. A home where flying fists and verbal abuse had been as commonplace as the stale, infested oatmeal he'd been expected to choke down at the breakfast table, or the freezing showers he was forced to take just so his foster parents could save the euros they'd greedily accepted from the government and kept for themselves.

Approaching his bedroom now, to where she'd marched off to rescue her shoes and whatever else she'd brought aboard on her little stowaway adventure, Nelios fully expected to toss her out and let the authorities charge her with whatever crime they saw fit.

Seeing her distraught expression when he entered, though, he hesitated. Not because he felt for her; absolutely not. But part of him wanted to understand how she could be so conclusively fooled. How her belief in Agnes and Tolis could be so unshakeable. *He* had known his parents were lying that day. And, true to their lies, they'd never bothered to come back for him. Not the year after, and not in the two decades since.

And yes, Vayle's knee-jerk offer to 'do anything' also intrigued him far more than he should've allowed. Even now, all the possibilities of how he could wield those two words in his favour seductively stirred through him.

His late father had had a gifted tongue, able to charm

the very birds from trees. What lies had he and Agnes spun on this woman? Was it even worth his time to try and disabuse her of her beliefs?

No. It wasn't. This interest was akin to a scientific experiment he wanted to comprehend, so he could actively avoid its deficiencies.

She was staring out of the window, at the hive of activity below. At the authorities who would shortly cart her away.

Nelios leaned against the doorway, a sliver of interest piercing his rigid guard. Her hair had almost fully escaped the knot at the back of her head, several heavy strands of rich chestnut battling with gravity to stay put. It drew attention to the sleek line of her neck, her slim shoulders and the tiny movement of her throat as she swallowed.

She sucked in a breath through parted lips and Nelios recalled her unguarded expression when he'd turned. The tiny flicker of her tongue ignited that same spark low in his belly, his jaw gritting as the spark gravitated south. No. He was absolutely not attracted to Apostolis's and Agnes's deluded little charity case.

And yet, when she took another, deeper breath, his gaze followed it to her firm breasts straining against the cheap suit she'd attempted to use as a disguise. Nelios cursed as the spark flamed higher.

'If you've come here to gloat, just get on with it, will you? You're running out of time.'

She kept her gaze on the window for several more seconds before pivoting to face him. The sight of her fighting tears while her chin lifted in clear defiance should have been laughable. But he wasn't laughing. He was wondering why the words he needed to utter remained locked in his throat. Why the two reasons continued to clamour ever louder as he slowly approached her.

Step aside. Cut her loose. Be done with this. Nelios shook his head, his brow furrowing tighter.

She blew out a breath, half-relieved, half-puzzled. Then, still eyeing him, she attempted to sidle past him. He would probably not understand why his hand shot out then, any time soon. Why he gripped her elbow to stop her taking another step. And why he gave life to the words that fell from his lips in that moment.

'I will stay your execution—not because of your entirely foolish offer to do anything, although we will revisit that later.'

Her eyes grew wide and, this close, Nelios saw the ocean-blue held green and gold specks that sparkled and dimmed at will. They could almost have been considered mesmerising if one were foolish enough to succumb to their allure.

'What do you want in return?'

A science experiment. That is all this is. Information gathering too. Knowledge is power, right?

'You're coming to Argentina with me. Make no mistake, your dilemma hasn't changed. With a single phone call I can have you thrown in jail and then deported, a process that could last weeks or months. You'll be in no position to help Agnes then. Or I will offer you an alternative: for the next forty-eight hours, you'll tell me everything I wish to know about them. And you will leave nothing out. Agreed?'

On the one hand, it felt like the easiest thing in the world to agree to. But Vayle knew that, scratch the surface, there were all sorts of traps waiting for the unsuspecting. Traps that could well give him the ammunition he sought against Agnes, the mother he believed had wronged him.

If she was going to agree to this she would have to play

this very carefully—and from the appearance of Nelios's right-hand man in the doorway, she knew her time was up, just as she knew prison in a foreign country was the very last thing she wanted.

'Why do you want to know about them? I thought you didn't care.'

His jaw clenched tightly, once. 'That is my business, not yours.'

She searched his features for some humanity. Vayle was reminded that he'd helped her with her cramp, despite coming across as ruthless and unfeeling. He'd fed her when he could easily have had her removed from his presence. But a trap was still a trap, whether disguised with flowers or lined with barbed wire. So she pushed just that little bit harder. 'Your illusions were shattered so you want mine shattered too? Because what—misery loves company?'

'Should it be an illusion to expect the people who decided to sire you to give you a modicum of care and consideration?'

The memory of being locked in a dark room for hours on end threatened to upsurge her already rollercoaster emotions. 'No, it's not. But expecting me to view my history through your warped lens is equally inconsiderate.' She raised her chin. 'But I will accept your deal. And, by the end of it, you'll see nothing you say can sway me about Tolis and Agnes.'

His mouth twisted, along with a hint of angst crossing his face, swiftly stifled. 'Tolis. How benign you make him sound. When exactly did he start calling himself that?'

The bitterness in his voice shook her to the core. 'I always knew him as Tolis. And I wasn't quite finished. I will accept your deal on condition that nothing I say will be used in this…vendetta against Agnes.'

The snort came from behind him, from Andreas. But Nelios raised his hand before his friend could put his clearly incredulous feelings into words. 'You're very bad at your job if you believe I'd need a lowly marketing and PR manager of a three-star hotel to give me the dirt I need to best my enemies. No, Miss Lancaster, I will not give you my word because it isn't needed. Agree without conditions or get the hell off my plane.'

Time ticked loudly and ominously in her head. Andreas levelled a narrow-eyed gaze at her, almost daring her not to take the deal. It was clear the other man despised her, that he wanted her gone.

In some abstract part of her brain she wondered what his story was; what exactly the two men had been through together. But she corralled her wayward thoughts. She was on the brink of buying herself two days, which was much longer than she'd anticipated when she'd hightailed it to London City airport half a day ago with her passport and a leaky plan with more holes in it than Swiss cheese.

She refocused on Nelios, on the laser beam gaze fixed squarely on her.

For better or worse... 'Yes. Agreed.'

CHAPTER THREE

HE REMAINED STILL, watching her for another taut stretch before he turned and nodded briskly at Andreas. The other man left without another word. And mere minutes later the police were gone, the refuelling truck had pulled away and the pilot had reboarded.

From her very shaky position as a stowaway, Vayle was elevated one tiny rung to unwanted guest, Nelios barely glancing at her as he instructed the head attendant to show her around. After a five-minute tour around the jaw-dropping double-floored aircraft, she was ushered into a tiny cabin.

'Mr Petralis advises you to rest for a few hours. You'll be summoned when he needs you.' The same attendant who'd brought her dinner hesitated for a moment before he pointed to the button. 'If you need anything, you can call me on that.'

He started to turn away but, cringing, Vayle stepped forward. 'Is there a way to make a phone call?'

'There is a way but Mr Petralis wishes any calls to be made in his presence.' Vayle opened her mouth to enquire why but he beat her to it. 'He says it's "part of the deal".'

Her lips pursed but she nodded. She suspected Nelios would trot out many more conditions in a bid to get her to back down, withholding her ability to contact Agnes probably high on the list.

Alone, she dropped down onto the single, perfectly made bed and glanced around her. Like everything else, it was top notch with bespoke accents and Nelios monograms stamped on the sheets and furniture. Trailing her finger over the silver jacquard coverlet, she once again wondered who was telling the truth in this scenario. If Tolis and Agnes had indeed abandoned their own child, could she cope with that knowledge? One tormentor for a parent was bad enough, but another two who had pulled the wool over her eyes...

No. Knowing she couldn't rest without letting Agnes know she was all right, she searched for her bag—because Nelios and his rules could go hang—only to remember that she'd discarded her phone somewhere on his bedroom floor. And regaining entry would be impossible this time round.

With a huff of impatience, she tossed off her shoes and climbed into the bed. While she hated to admit he was right, exhaustion sucked at her limbs, the tumultuous few hours she'd had suddenly weighing down on her. Tugging the coverlet off the high-thread-count sheets, she crawled under the covers and within minutes she fell asleep, the sound of the engine lulling her.

The firm knock on the door dragged her out of sleep what felt like only minutes later. Jerking upright, she stumbled out of bed and went to the door. The same attendant waited on the other side, his impassive face not drawing attention to the fact that she must've looked a horror.

'I suppose Mr Petralis wants to see me?' she asked.

'No. I came to tell you we will be landing in ten minutes, so you should put your seat belt on.'

'What? But we've only been flying for a couple of hours.'

'We've been in the air for seven hours, Miss Lancaster, and you've been asleep for most of them.'

She frowned at the darkened windows, expecting to see sunlight if what he was saying was true. Then she paused when he reached for the little nub next to the light switch, pressed it and the window shades changed.

'The windows are regulated to maximise rest.'

She bit her lip, knowing it wasn't his fault she'd been so tired she'd slept like the dead in the best bedding she'd ever experienced in her life.

'Thank you, I'll be ready,' she said.

With a brisk nod, he left again.

Knowing her restful state was temporary and would most likely be reversed the moment she was in Nelios's presence—because the man only needed to breathe to remind everyone in his vicinity that he was an apex predator—she went into the adjoining bathroom. There, presented with an array of luxurious products that probably cost more than the entire stock of accessories at Vayle Hotel, she set about freshening up as best she could.

Done, she pulled open the door to find the attendant waiting in the hallway. She took a closer look at him and realised he looked large and intimidating enough to double up as a bodyguard. And, come to think of it, every member of the crew looked different from the run-of-the mill ones she encountered on a normal commercial flight.

She was wondering about that when she was led into the main cabin. Her belly did that crazy somersault when she zeroed in on Nelios. He too had freshened up. His slightly damp hair was styled off his forehead, his clean shave throwing his square jaw and dimpled chin into relief. The suit he wore to the meeting had been swapped for a navy version, the dark shirt underneath making his warm, olive skin glow in a way that made her fingers tingle with the urge to touch... Was she insane?

She realised the thought had frozen her whole body when his eyes slid from Andreas to rest on her, one eyebrow quirked. 'Do you plan to break a few more rules by remaining standing while we land, Miss Lancaster?'

Galvanised by his electric voice and her own impatience with herself and her behaviour around this man, she hurried to the nearest available seat as she spotted the tops of buildings just outside the window. She'd barely clipped herself in when the wheels touched down.

Moments later, Nelios followed by Andreas and the crew disembarked like a well-oiled machine and headed for the fleet of cars awaiting them. Feeling like the ugly duckling in a veritable gaggle of swans, she hurried to keep up, darting towards the tinted-windowed SUV the attendant indicated. Hugely relieved not to see any sign of the police, she slid into the back of the vehicle...and lost the breath she'd just taken when she came face-to-face with Nelios.

Of course he wouldn't want her out of his sight. Her heartbeat further escalated when she realised they were alone, with the privacy partition fully in place.

'I'm guessing you want to start your interrogation right away?' she said into the tense silence.

'Considering you've had what accounts to a full night's sleep? Yes, I do believe I should make hay before you whittle away all my time.'

She licked her lower lip, then tensed when he followed the action with narrowed, heated eyes. 'All right, then, what do you want to know?'

Silence reigned. Her heart thumped loudly in her ears. When full minute had passed, and his nostrils had flared once, twice, as if he sought control, Vayle forced herself not to squirm.

'You claim they are your "surrogate parents".'

'I'm not hearing a question there.' She was hedging for time. She shouldn't have been surprised he'd plunged right into the deep end. Yet she'd been unprepared to have her anguish over her father's illness, known only to a handful of people, pried open so starkly.

'Did they *unofficially* adopt you?' he went on coldly, his sneer over the word making her heart lurch. 'Was it part of the bank's terms when they took over?'

A wave of light-headedness washed over her. 'What do you know about the…about that?'

His speaking look questioned her reasoning, mocking why she would ask it in the first place. 'The bank's terms were private.'

'You truly believe there's such a thing as privacy when you're in the thick of a hostile takeover?'

'If you have any semblance of humanity, yes.'

He delivered a cold, hard smile that froze her middle. 'And, as we've established, I have none. So answer the question.'

'And if I refuse?'

'Then I would deem you extremely foolish for backing out on a deal you've made with me. You're not an ally by a long shot, but you definitely don't want to become my enemy. So for starters, and for wasting several hours of my time, I'll drive you to the police station myself.'

She swallowed, partly glad her frozen status had halted her squirming. It was also easier for her numbed senses when she answered. 'Yes and no. Yes, there was no official documentation, and no, it wasn't a specific requirement by the bank. But it was approved by the doctors who…' She paused, pressed her lips together and watched his face for signs that he knew more about her past. About the true reasons that had necessitated Tolis's and Agnes's stable presence in her life.

'The doctors who first diagnosed your father?' he finished, much to her horror.

He knew. Nelios knew at least something about her father's condition. The condition George Lancaster had point blank refused to have treated, subjecting her and anyone who encountered the Lancaster family to needless distress.

It was only after her father's diagnosis of depression and acute mania had been discovered—an extreme version of his bipolar disorder—on the request of the bank who held the mortgage on his precious Vayle Hotel, and their subsequent insistence on his receiving treatment and donating power of attorney that he'd agreed to seek help. And, even then, he'd defied the recommended treatment at every turn.

She dragged her gaze away because she didn't want to know if Nelios knew more. Did he know the extent of her father's neglect of her—the distance between father and daughter that Vayle had never been able to close following her mother's death when she'd been ten? George Lancaster had fallen apart in the aftermath, his grief and depression driving him into bouts of careless cruelty and unreliability.

Gritting her teeth against the surge of rough emotions, Vayle exhaled. 'Yes.' It was a mere whisper, but she knew he heard it.

His piercing gaze didn't relent. 'What were the bank's conditions, precisely?'

'Don't you already know?'

'Not yet,' he replied. 'But I will once I own Vayle Hotel.'

She chanced a glance at him and saw the rigid control he'd fastened over his emotions. Whereas only a handful of hours ago she'd marvelled at it, Vayle now wondered how much effort it took for Nelios Petralis to keep all that willpower in place.

'So you're really going ahead with this takeover? Do you care who you hurt in the process?'

His jaw rippled and her thought deepened. *Why did he need to exert so much control? What was buried beneath his glacial surface?*

'Everyone involved besides you and Agnes will be offered compensation and a position elsewhere. And you, as owner, are being paid more than market value for a crumbling relic. I'd hardly call that hurting you. What you're really asking is if this is personal to Agnes Adamis. The answer is yes, it is. So, as agreed, you will tell me what I wish to know,' he tagged on silkily. *Like the cobra said to the mouse.*

Vayle considered refusing; considered using that information to strike a better deal. But if felt...sleazy to use her family trauma, *her very personal* trauma, as a bargaining tool. Besides, as he'd so arrogantly announced, if she failed in this task—and that hope dwindled by the second—he would have the sordid details presented to him on a silver platter anyway.

'My father had a condition that went undiagnosed for years.' She curled her fists in her lap, the admission tunnelling to the very heart of her painful memories. 'Severe mood swings that arose out of nowhere, lingered for hours, then disappeared. My mother, when she was alive, was the only one he'd listen to. She would cover for him—pacify the guests he offended.' A bitter smile twisted her lips until she forced it away. 'Unfortunately, after her death, he...fell apart. And with social media, and information now readily available, word started to spread about Dad's condition and the hotel started to suffer. As you probably know, we were mortgaged to the hilt.'

'Why didn't the bank foreclose straight away if it was a losing business?' he asked curiously.

She shook her head. 'The bank manager was Dad's friend. He kept giving him a chance to turn things round. And, at first, he would. When he wasn't feeling…himself he would let the junior staff take over, that sort of thing. But inevitably things would take a turn for the worse…until eventually the bank gave him an ultimatum. He could stay on as the owner and proprietor on the condition he hired a manager and assistant to run the day to day.' Her gaze darted to him to catch a wave of bleak bitterness.

'And did the bank insist that these people your father hired were to be childless or did he come up with that condition on his own?' His voice was tinder-dry and bitter.

Her heart lurched again and, although she suspected the awful answer, having lived with George Lancaster almost all her life, she answered with the truth. 'No bank has the right to order that. I think it was my father. I had no idea that stipulation even existed before you mentioned it today.'

Again those dark-brown eyes bore into her, digging out her hidden depths. Staring back, she caught a shadow of what he felt. It wasn't enough to trigger a sense of kinship but it…eased one tiny knot inside her.

'Continue,' he said, his tone back to that chilled edge with the many complex emotions weaved in.

'As I said, it wasn't official, but they were a great help—they taught me everything they knew about running a hotel.' She shrugged. 'I had a father who was indifferent to whether I was sick or healthy, fed or hungry. They… saved me from the worst parts of his neglect.'

A sound that was part-growl part-scoff rumbled from

him, freezing her words. 'The documents show you're the rightful heir to Vayle Hotel. That your father dying without a will means you would've inherited it after the issues with the bank were resolved.'

She didn't hide her glare. 'Are you insinuating that the only reason your parents helped me was because they wanted the hotel I would eventually own?'

'They are *not* my parents,' he delivered acidly through his teeth. 'And no, it's not an insinuation, it's a fact.'

She opened her mouth to hotly refute that. Only to startle when her car door was pulled open and she turned to find a doorman standing attention with a welcoming smile on his face.

They'd arrived.

Amongst the stylish gems littered around the impressive Recoleta neighbourhood of Buenos Aires, including the Four Seasons and other high-end hotels, the Rosa Corona was a cut above the rest.

But even it couldn't hold a candle to the nearly finished hotel right across the street from it. Nelios XV, the soon-to-be crown jewel in Nelios Petralis's collection, had been whispered about on the luxury hotel circuit for the better part of three years. It was rumoured that the elite suites didn't just come with butlers and top chefs, but that the experience would include a private jet, a yacht and chefs flown across the world at a word. Put simply, to live the Nelios XV experience would be to inhabit a world where every single whim was catered for without exception—at the kind of price tag double the GDP of most small countries.

Vayle stood at her hotel room window in the suite adjoining the one Nelios had disappeared into the second they'd stepped off the lift. Looking across at the breathtaking architecture of the nearly finished hotel, she found herself once again wondering if the kind of motivation it took to birth not just one but fifteen masterpieces so far—and counting—was part of Nelios's DNA or a characteristic formed out of the trauma he'd undergone.

If it was true.

But...why would he lie? He'd all but succeeded in his plans to destroy Vayle Hotel and force a buyout. They'd already been on the back foot for a few years, barely making the payments to the bank after the deaths of both her father and Tolis, before Nelios's new hotel had sprung up directly next to them—all glitz and elegance, sucking the life out of the woefully-in-need-of-refurbishment Vayle Hotel. Their bookings had taken a steep dive, requiring them to take out emergency funding from the bank just to keep their heads above water.

While Vayle's marketing ideas had seen a few surges in bookings, to her horror their rival had immediately countered their efforts, even going as far as to drastically slash their prices. She'd been puzzled as to why they would do that, until Agnes had tearfully confessed her relationship with Nelios. Things had gone steadily downhill from then on.

She shivered in recollection at his icy loathing when he'd seen Agnes at that meeting yesterday. No. That sort of reaction hadn't been manufactured. Which meant...something had gone drastically wrong somewhere.

Her chest tightening at the implications, she turned away from the view of the hotel even she couldn't deny was simply extraordinary. Like its namesake hotels across the world, the front edifice was sculpted in glass, grey stone and steel around the distinct Roman numerals, making it stand out, while also blending into the historical architecture. It was a soaring building that would repeatedly draw the eye with the promise of discovering a new feature with each glance. Vayle grimaced at the bite of envy of whomever would get the privilege of working within its walls when the ping from her phone refocused her attention.

She'd tried to call Agnes the second she was alone but she hadn't picked up. Snatching up her phone now, she read the text from Agnes.

Are you okay? I'm worried about you. Text an update when you can.

Her heart warming, and roiling emotions settling, she immediately dialled again. Then frowned when it rang and went to voicemail.

The time difference was only three hours ahead in England. Vayle wondered why she hadn't picked up. Clearing her throat, she left a message, attempting not to sound as perturbed as she felt. She decided that probing deeper about why Agnes had lost touch with her son, the man actively trying to destroy them, was a conversation she would prefer to have in person. She knew there was a measure of shying away from the possible truth but she grasped at the distraction when a knock sounded on her door.

Setting her phone on the coffee table, she went to open it, to see the head attendant from the plane, now dressed in a sharp suit with a visible bulge at his waist that confirmed his dual role as bodyguard.

'Hello,' she offered tentatively. 'I'm sorry, I don't know your name.'

'It's Capaldi,' he said. 'Mr Petralis would like you to join him for dinner in an hour.'

'Oh…um, sure.' She glanced past him then grimaced at the futility of it. 'Where?'

'In his suite. One floor up. I will come and fetch you.'

'Thanks.' She shut the door, then glanced down at herself. She looked and felt grimy. She'd intended to shower, but she couldn't stomach wearing the same clothes she'd been wearing for twenty-four hours straight. Recalling the shops she'd seen downstairs, she made a quick decision and grabbed her bag.

Funds were scarce, and she'd taken a drastic income cut from the hotel when their troubles had started, but she'd barely touched the rainy day savings from the small inheritance her mother had left her. And, while she was severely on the back foot when it came to her interactions with Nelios Petralis, she could at least continue from a place of better confidence.

Vayle blew out a relieved breath when she made it downstairs without encountering either Andreas or Capaldi. She'd been half-afraid they'd appear like a nightmare and inform her she was to stay in her room until Nelios gave her express permission to leave. Was he so confident she'd stay put—that he had her exactly where he wanted her?

Yes. Unfortunately.

Mildly grumpy at the thought, she entered the hotel boutique and just as quickly exited when the eye-watering prices and disdainful looks told her she was out of her league.

The warm sultry air, even at that time of the evening, was welcome as she hurried towards the brighter lights that, thankfully, produced shops in her price range.

Within fifteen minutes she'd secured dark indigo jeans, stylish enough to pass muster as smart-casual, and two tops: one a sleeveless black satin peplum and the other a flowery lilac billow-sleeved blouse she could wear during the day. Her kitten heels would work with both. Adding a couple of accessories and paying quickly, she hightailed it back to her suite and into the shower.

She tidied her hair into a loose bun with a compact hairbrush, and she was halfway through pulling on her clothes when the knock sounded. Buttoning her jeans, she caught up the hook earrings and managed to secure one, only to get flustered when the other one refused to situate in her lobe.

The knock came again, more insistently.

Stifling a curse, she rushed towards the door. 'I'm coming!'

Still attempting to do up the side-zip of her top *and* slide one hoop in her ear, she gave up with the earring, turned the handle and immediately turned away. 'I'll be another minute, Capaldi. Sorry, time got away from me.' She tried a second time, blew out a breath when she got the hoop into her ear, then tackled the zip once more.

At the taut silence, she frowned over her shoulder.

Nelios stood tall and imposing in the doorway, darkbrown eyes fixed squarely on her. A shudder slammed out of nowhere, rippling through her body.

Shock—it was shock—*not* sizzling awareness with a heavy dose of electricity that gripped her very core and rattled it mercilessly.

'Oh, I thought you were Capaldi.'

'That is apparent.' His searing scrutiny and biting tone froze her as he stepped into the room and shut the door, her hand still on the zip of the top that half-gaped, displaying the side edges of her bra. Face flaming when his gaze tracked her from top to bottom, she twisted away and tried to finish what should've been a simple task but had instead become an arduous challenge.

'Are you in the habit of letting men into your room while half-dressed?' he asked.

She snorted. 'Hardly. And you didn't have to come in, did you? Or be so impatient?'

Her answer clearly didn't please him. His eyes narrowed, the expression in them blazing to life at her continued wriggling. 'What are you doing?'

Was his voice raspier or was it just the buzzing in her ears? Another wave of heat washed over her as she was forced to admit, 'My zip is stuck. I think.' *Damn it.* If it didn't budge, there was no way she could get it off. And she could hardly go to dinner half-dressed, could she?

Cringing, she faced him. 'Could you...could you help me?'

One brow quirked, and he said nothing for uncomfortably long seconds. Then, prowling closer, he nudged his square chin at her. She released the pull tab and kept her arm aloft. Did she wish the ground would open and swallow her? Very much so.

Somehow she managed to keep her chin up and he studied her.

'I'll have to insert a finger to protect your skin.' His voice was lower, definitely with a deeper rasp, and she dragged her gaze up to find his rising from her side to rest on her face. This close, his brown eyes didn't look so dark and ominous. They looked...warm; heated, even, with dark-gold specks that made them glint as he waited for her response.

'O-okay.' *Dear heaven.* Could she sound more breathless?

The sight of his large hands and elegant fingers tackling her delicate zip shouldn't have been erotic. Shouldn't have made heat pool low in her belly or simmer between her legs. And yet there she was—dying and praying he would mistake the tiny shivers coursing through her for something else. Nelios's knuckles brushing the skin over her ribs shouldn't have been more than a ticklish sensation. Instead, Vayle became abruptly aware of an erogenous zone she'd had no inkling of before today.

She bit back a moan as her very skin jerked and shivered. Her peaking nipples were unmistakable through the shiny satin. The rise and fall of her chest blared her agitation.

'Easy. You need to remain still, Vayle,' he murmured.

Oh, God. It was impossible, she wanted to protest. Between the deeper gruffness of his voice, the faintly accented way his voice curled out her name and the new sensation of his masculine scent filtering through her senses, she had to shut her eyes to contain her wayward reactions.

'It is done,' he said curtly.

She took a giant sidestep as she opened her eyes, attempting to blink reason into her sluggish brain. 'T-thank you.' Another step. 'I'll be…' She looked around for her phone and, spotting it where she'd left it on the coffee table, rushed across to snatch it up. A quick glance showed Agnes hadn't returned her call. Stemming another tendril of worry, she sucked in a breath and faced him. 'I'm ready.'

Again he watched her for several more seconds than was strictly polite, his aura deceptively calm, a technique she was learning was very effective in disarming his opponents. Thank goodness she would not be in his orbit for very much longer.

Then, without a word, he turned and strode for the door. She followed him, watching him activate the lift with a special keycard and, when it arrived, he stood to one side to let her enter.

Still wordless, they rode up one floor.

Vayle was stunned all over again by the plush surroundings. But, before she could take in any specific details, Andreas walked towards them, a neutral expression that belied the mild censure in his gaze as he exchanged words in Greek with Nelios before he eyed her.

'Enjoy your evening,' he said with a distinct lack of sincerity that made her grimace.

'Is it even worth asking why he dislikes me so much or should I save my breath?' she asked Nelios once the doors had shut behind Andreas.

He paused in the wide, exquisitely decorated hallway. 'We share a dislike for wilful blindness,' he delivered, before striding deeper into the suite.

Ouch.

On slow feet, she followed him into the lavish suite past groupings of sofas and an extensive bar area, through an alcove to an elegant dining table set for two. It wasn't lost on her at all that through the floor-to-ceiling windows, displayed in perfect lighting, was the Nelios XV.

At every turn he meant to remind her who he was, what their association meant. As if she could forget, when her every breath, her every erratic heartbeat, shrieked how far out of her comfort zone she was.

He pulled out her chair and she sat down. She startled a little and earned herself a narrow-eyed look when his hand brushed her bare skin.

'Why so jumpy?'

She shrugged. 'Guess I'm waiting for the hammer to fall. Or for the interrogation to resume.'

He took his own seat, his mouth turning down with mild derision. 'Hardly a hammer when I let you roam freely in the streets earlier on, shopping without a care in the world.'

'Let me...?' she echoed, then frowned. 'How do you know where I went? Are you having me followed?'

'You're here in my care. Besides the fact that I and anyone in my group are required to use a security team, and you traipsed out without so much as a whisper to anyone, you have already proven not to have the best judgement with your stowaway antics. Do you truly believe I'm not within my rights to keep tabs on you? Let's not forget that you're also in this country illegally and I will be culpable should you be discovered.'

'Does it make you feel powerful to list everyone's weaknesses or it a safeguarding crutch?' she enquired softly, ignoring her sprinting pulse, which she was one hundred per cent confident was fully derived from anger, not hopelessness.

He stiffened so hard, he resembled marble. 'Excuse me?'

She sighed. 'My use of the word "hammer" before wasn't an exaggeration, it seems. You Hulk-smash when a scalpel is needed.'

One dark brow arched, drawing her attention to the sinfully silky length of his sooty lashes. 'Are you accusing me of lacking finesse, Vayle?'

'Maybe I am... Nelios.'

His nostrils flared—because he was irritated, right? Not because he was reacting to the cursed breathlessness that had made her sound like a cheesy movie siren when she'd said his name. The live wire that seemed to need no encouragement at all to zing to life writhed through her. Fiercely combating it, she picked up her napkin and took her time spreading it over thighs that had grown far too hot, scaldingly aware he was staring at her. About to snap at his rudeness, her breath stalled as a door opened to the side and a man dressed in chef's whites accompanied by a butler bearing wine pushed in a sterling-silver trolley.

'Good evening, Mr Petralis, Miss Lancaster,' they both greeted.

She blinked. Had Nelios bothered to tell the chef her name? She murmured a response then listened as the chef rattled off the mouthwatering menu he'd prepared. Spoilt for choice, she picked the first thing she remembered and was presented with a sumptuous Greek salad drizzled with olive oil. Then she proceeded to stifle moan after moan while she ate the most glorious melt-in-the-mouth empanadas she'd ever tasted, accompanied by sublime red wine.

Surprisingly, Nelios didn't grill her over dinner. But she saw his gaze repeatedly linger on the phone she'd placed on the dining table. Etiquette-wise, it wasn't strictly polite, but Vayle hadn't wanted to miss a call.

He waited until she was done with her decadent dessert before he struck. 'Have you been in touch with Agnes to report your progress?'

'What progress? All you've done is threaten to have me thrown in jail.' She bit the inside of her cheek, because that wasn't strictly true. Yes he'd threatened her, but he'd also given her a choice. And she'd accepted. 'What I mean is—'

'I'm well aware of what you mean. You're much more comfortable listing all the bad things perpetrated on you and blithely ignoring the good.'

She flushed, then was inexorably drawn to study him when she heard the underlying bleakness in his voice. But his face was shut tighter than Fort Knox. And, since she was swimming in a shallow pond of her own disingenuousness, she remained silent.

Until, 'Answer the question, Vayle,' he insisted firmly.

And, yes, this time she couldn't deny that she shivered

solely because of the way he said her name with a gravelly bite that seemed to rake over her jittery senses, sending waves of heat and awareness through her body.

'No, I haven't spoken to your…to Agnes. She texted. I tried calling back but there was no answer.'

His gaze bore into her. 'What exactly did the text say?'

'To find out how I am because she hadn't heard from me and is worried,' she answered unequivocally.

Something darted across his face, hot and fast as quicksilver. It was indecipherable then gone…but not forgotten. It was visceral enough to strike her hard in the middle.

'That wasn't all, though, was it?' came the hard, sardonic rejoinder. As if he needed there to be more.

She lifted her eyebrows. 'Because you want there to be? Something that justifies your beliefs?'

He didn't rise to her bait, merely levelled his incisive gaze on her and waited until it wore her down, leaving her no choice but to respond.

'Yes; she also asked if I had any updates.'

And then that mocking smile appeared. It was full-bodied, labelling her ten kinds of a fool for believing that the warmth and affection she'd treasured for years had been genuine. That the surrogate mother—who'd kept her aloft when she'd thought she would drown in her father's cruelty and disregard, both before and after his diagnosis—was not who Vayle believed her to be.

That his smile was devastatingly gorgeous shouldn't have factored in at all. And yet her runaway heartbeat howled and said otherwise—that her inability to look away from his magnificent face or to control the sizzling heat rising within her was a big problem. Huge. Because she intensely disliked the narrative Nelios was attempting to force her to face. *And* he warped her brain with this chemistry between them that she couldn't deny.

Tossing her napkin on the table, she snatched up her phone and marched into the living room. There she stopped and spun round...to catch his fiery gaze on her backside.

Her heated demand dried up. *What the hell had she been about to say?* So she stood there, caught in that insane vortex of awareness as he slowly rose and sauntered towards her. A clutch of words peppered her sluggish brain as she tried to stop staring at his raw, masculine body. 'Where do you want me?' she blurted.

His stride hitched a tiny fraction, and he inhaled sharply. 'What?'

Oh, yes. She truly wished for a lethal lightning bolt instantly to destroy her.

'For your interrogation. Where should I...can I...sit?' she amended.

'Dangling you from the ceiling by your fingernails so soon after dinner is too tedious, so by all means, yes, sit down, Vayle.' He gestured at the nearest group of sofas.

She chose the furthest sofa, ignoring the twitch of mockery on his face as he sat at the other end, suavely crossing one leg over the other.

The butler approached and Nelios turned to her. 'Nightcap?'

She started to shake her head, then at the last moment she nodded. 'Please.' Glancing at the butler, she smiled. 'Surprise me.' She'd learned very early that hospitality staff loved demonstrating their skills and, from the butler's pleased nod, she'd guessed right.

He returned minutes later with an amber-coloured drink for Nelios and a bright-yellow drink for her. He hovered as she took a sip, blinked and took a larger sip.

'This is lovely; thank you so much.'

His broader smile warmed her like the clementine-based alcoholic drink in her hand.

'If you're quite done?' Nelios drawled.

She eyed him as the butler left. 'Clearly you don't believe that when you make people feel valued they repay you in ways you might not expect.'

He set his glass on his raised knee. 'Another lesson from…those people?'

'Yes, as a matter of fact.'

He looked poleaxed for a flash, then openly sceptical. 'Next you're going to tell me they hung the moon,' he drawled in a voice coated with acid.

'I'm not going to volunteer anything you don't emphatically ask for, because I'll be wasting my breath. So…' she took another sip of her drink then cradled her glass in her palm '…fire away.'

CHAPTER FOUR

It was almost laughable how unequivocal she was in her beliefs. How intransigently she clung to her well-disguised monsters.

Almost.

As Nelios examined this strange woman—who should've been easy enough to dismiss but somehow clung burr-like in his head—he wondered why he was even bothering. Clearly, she'd been brainwashed to slavishly fall for the lines she'd been fed. A coating of sugar disguised the poison pill.

He'd read the thorough report his well-paid sources had provided on the history of Vayle Hotel and its owner. He knew George Lancaster had been a living nightmare: a minor aristocrat clinging doggedly to what remained of a family estate he'd whittled away through careless dealings, and an arrogant refusal to seek help with a condition that could've been managed with a little care and attention.

Equally careless was the child he'd dragged into the middle of his tumultuous, woefully mismanaged life. For a while, Vayle's mother had helped, but she'd died too soon, leaving her child in the clutches of yet another monster.

His mouth twisted. This was one of the many reasons he wanted neither a wife nor children. Hell, it was why his rigorously controlled policy of seven days of dinner, sex—if both parties were willing—and a fond, tasteful, gift-strewn farewell was so successful. A policy he'd *never* once strayed from, long before he'd made his first million. It was why he'd even contemplated having a vasectomy, to remove the last risk of ever parenting a child and passing on the monstrous strain of cruelty Apostolis and Agnes might have bequeathed to him. Nelios wasn't entirely sure why he'd allowed Andreas to talk him out of that decision. But, no matter, with his system firmly in place, there would be no risk anyway.

Apparently, though, Vayle's treatment from her father had driven her into his parents' arms, them readily providing the saviour status they'd needed to trap her into a long, lucrative arrangement. No other explanation made sense.

So why are you digging any further?

He ignored the voice and watched her sip the drink his pleased butler had made her. Shifting in his seat when another wave of disgruntlement attacked his spine, he prodded the scab he was sure hid no festering wound. It couldn't. It'd calcified a long time ago. As he'd told himself before, this was merely a matter of him learning his enemies' ways.

'How old are you, Vayle?'

Luminous blue eyes landed on his and blinked, searched. 'Why?'

'You earned a scholarship and have a degree in hospitality and marketing from a respectable university.' His gaze moved over her, attempting not to recall how smooth her warm skin had felt beneath his fingers when he'd helped her with her zip. How her repeated breath-catching had threatened the edges of his control. *How much he wanted to touch her again.* 'You seem old enough to have taken over the helm of the hotel which bears your name. Why haven't you?'

'First of all, I'm twenty-six. And why don't you ask me what you really mean—why haven't I tossed Agnes out onto the streets like you claim they did to you?' She shook her head and, while his gut clenched hard with each utterance of his mother's name, heat pooled lower when his attention was drawn to the mouth pursing then twisting with displeasure at his questions.

Maybe this was truly a fool's errand. Maybe he should just leave her blind and naively trusting, waiting for the buy-out to reach its final and acceptable outcome. Let her see how quickly she would be dropped by the woman she believed had her back. How devastatingly alone and cold the world would turn when Agnes walked away as callously from her as she'd walked away from him.

Feeling the bitter and cold fingers of desolation reach for him, he slammed those emotions back where they belonged—in the vault clearly marked *never, ever again*. He'd risen above those first shocking days and weeks of realising he was nothing but a pay cheque to those who should've cared that a twelve-year-old boy had two perfectly healthy parents who still walked the earth but had actively chosen to offload him like a piece of lost luggage just so they could pursue a greater ambition in life.

Hell, he'd even dug deep enough to kill the tears that had threatened after his third or fourth slap across the face when he'd spoken out for himself and other mistreated children under his foster parents' roof. And the scales had long fallen off his eyes when he'd decided he'd be better off alone on the streets than remain in foster care any longer.

Nelios reminded himself how far he'd come. How those

tricky few weeks had been the test he'd needed to reforge himself into something unbreakable, untouchable.

These days he surrounded himself with men and women who'd been through similar challenges. Such as Andreas; such as Capaldi. Every single person who held a position of note in his empire knew what it was like to suffer hardship. To go hungry for days. To fight in the darkest pits of hell. To know how to suffer bruise on top of bruise on top of inhumane humiliation and still keep going. They valued life, embraced the comforts of wealth and luxury but never forgot how easily it could all be stripped away, and they worked hard to ensure it never could be.

An apt tenet to live by if there was one.

So why are you revisiting the past?

'Indeed.' He realised he'd said it as much to himself as in response to her. 'You're right. That was what I was thinking. But I'm realising there's no point. You won't be convinced. And this subject has grown boring. You will be put on an aeroplane as soon as a flight is confirmed. I hope, for your sake, we never meet again.'

He knocked back the rest of his drink. This futile endeavour should've ended in Ascension when they'd stopped to refuel. Hell, it should never have started in London in the first place. He'd lowered his guard and allowed intrigue and, yes, his rare fascination with her, overrule his common sense. No more.

He uncrossed his leg and started to rise.

'Wait.'

Nelios wasn't sure why his gut tightened on hearing that husky imploration. Then he remembered when he'd heard it from her last; what she'd said immediately after that: *I'll do anything.* He hadn't yet tested that offer. He had dismissed it out of his mind because, as Andreas had scoffed, it was indeed a rookie mistake to offer such a thing to street-hardened predators such as them.

And yet... Nelios found himself doing as she'd asked: waiting; his senses on full alert and that pool of heat in his groin building, simmering.

She set down her glass and licked a drop of liquid from her bottom lip. 'How do I get you to reconsider what...what you plan to do?'

'It's very simple. You can't. Our association, such as it was, is over. Your hotel will be assessed for its viability and either subsumed as an annex to mine or disposed of.'

She shook her head so emphatically, silk strands slid against her nape. He wanted to touch that too. *Theos*. Was he so hard up? Frowning inwardly, he tried to remember the last time he'd had sex and was taken aback when he couldn't remember. Seriously, had it been that long?

'I refuse to accept that,' she said firmly.

Against his will, amusement trickled through him. Nelios abstractedly noted that she seemed to command varying sensations within him. He wanted to throw her into prison one moment, then wanted to crack a smile in the next. A ping from the phone in his pocket drew yet another emotion: irritation. Three feelings within three minutes. Most likely a record.

Drawing out his phone, he read the message:

Guests list confirmed and attached for the pre-launch party.

Even before he'd returned the phone to his pocket he'd made up his mind. 'You wish to attempt the futile?' he taunted.

Her plump lips pursed. 'I wish to keep talking. You said I had forty-eight hours. You not wanting to hear what

I have to say shouldn't change that. I have things to say to you, regardless.'

Again, he felt his mouth curve upward. He killed the motion. 'Your resilience, if nothing else, should prove interesting. The butler will see you out. Be ready to leave first thing in the morning.' He started to walk away, then paused. 'And Vayle?'

Her eyes widened a fraction. 'Hmm…yes?'

'I haven't forgotten that you said, "I'll do anything". And, believe me, I mean to test it.'

'Where are we?' Vayle asked as she wandered onto the widest enclosed terrace she'd ever seen in real life. She was learning 'real life' in Nelios Petralis's world was on a wildly different scale to hers.

She was a little shell-shocked by the dizzying speed of everything that had happened this morning. After a protracted tour of Nelios XV—which had far surpassed everything her imagination had conjured up where tasteful and even obscene luxury were concerned—they'd taken the super-speedy lift to the top of their hotel. There they'd boarded a sleek helicopter with Andreas, Capaldi and a handful of sharp-suited, sharp-eyed, tablet-wielding staff wearing menacing-looking earpieces.

They'd flown north, and upon landing the others had all immediately dispersed with almost robot-like efficiency, leaving her alone with Nelios. Vayle wasn't afraid to admit, she'd been a teensy bit intimidated by it all. But it dimmed beneath the sheer magnificence of their current location.

'A private estate that's been in the owner's family for generations,' Nelios answered. 'They're in dire straits and are thinking of selling. I'm considering adding it to the Nelios Group's portfolio but I haven't decided yet. My short stay here is a test run, of sorts.'

'Well, you should seriously consider it. It's stunning,' she breathed. And, when his gaze pivoted to her, Vayle wasn't even self-conscious about her blatant appreciation of the property. She shrugged and carried on. 'But I don't need to tell you that.'

'No, you don't. But I'm still interested in hearing your theories on how to best position this in a hospitality market,' he said.

'There's no such thing as free advice, Mr Petralis,' she half-joked.

She'd spent the night tossing and turning, swinging between guilt about wondering if Agnes was avoiding her because she bore some culpability, the way her son had accused, and reminding herself of the older woman's unfailing kindness to her over the years. Then, pushing away the unsettling sensation that thought brought, she'd attempted to plot how best to utilise the time she'd bought for herself. Why, given a second opportunity, she hadn't addressed that thinly veiled warning from Nelios about using her words against her. Hell, it was almost as if she wanted him to push her, just to see how far she would let him go…

Which was absurd. *Right?*

His face remained stoical. 'You're still convinced you can change my mind about your hotel's fate?' His voice held a little more bite, altering the atmosphere from taut to downright edgy.

Vayle's belly clenched but she fought to hang onto her composure. 'Maybe this should be less of a professional discourse and more of a personal, human one?'

He approached her slowly. Vayle told herself she remained where she was, and didn't obey her instinct to step back, because firstly it would show weakness—and she *wasn't* afraid of him, despite the wild fluttering in her belly and at her throat—and secondly because Nelios would respect her more if she met him on equal footing.

And, yes, she needed him to respect her. She'd withstood too much from her father and come out on the other side to allow her opinions and needs to be cast aside.

'Personal?' he echoed, his eyes now set to narrow-eyed sizzling as they trailed her from head to toe and back again. 'Is this where the "I'll do anything" is finally unleashed?' he enquired softly. *Lethally*.

'What…unleashed…? What are you talking about?'

Head tilted, his focus never once waned or altered. After another tense moment his mouth twisted and he stepped back. Did she think he intended to ease up on his imposing demands? Not by a long shot. 'You were saying about this place?'

She stared at him for a moment longer before forcing her brain to track with the abrupt change of subject and the peculiar, hollow sensation it'd left behind, almost as if a building anticipation had been dashed. Because it occurred to her now that she'd never quite taken back that ill-advised statement. Never stated categorically that she'd changed her mind and that, no, she wouldn't actually offer to 'do anything'.

So do it now. She inwardly shook her head. Doing it now would be ineffectual—bolting the door after the horse had fled. But when…*if*…it came back up, then she would make her feelings clear on the subject.

Realising he was still waiting for her response, she cleared her throat. 'There's a darling little village in France, barely two thousand acres, that people rent whole for various gatherings. This could be an uber-exclusive version of that. Throw in an excellent ground team, with prime activities and marketing to the super-elite where they're guaranteed they'll have the whole place to themselves, and not have to encounter another snooty billionaire, and you'll have them falling over themselves to jump onto your waiting list. You could be booked out for years.'

The edge had receded from his eyes by the time Vayle was finished, and he almost looked…impressed. Contemplative.

She couldn't stop the little fizz of pride that welled up inside her. At the very least, she could take heart in having distracted him from 'I'll do anything' that still dredged unfathomable feelings inside her.

'Interesting,' he muttered after a minute.

She raised her brows. 'Just…interesting? I challenge you to top that.'

One corner of his sensual lips quirked. 'I will not rise to the bait, alas. I pay eye-watering sums to far better marketing experts to provide me with innovative ideas.'

The fizz threatened to sputter out but she lifted her chin. 'Go ahead, then. I'll wait with bated breath to see what they come up with.'

For some reason that made his gaze drop to her mouth and made that same mouth tingle so wildly, her breath caught. And, between those two crazy reactions, they were frozen in a charged bubble of intense awareness when Andreas entered. They were still caught in it when he started to speak.

While her head buzzed with whatever the hell was happening to her, Nelios responded to his right-hand man without taking his eyes off her. It took a minute to realise that Andreas had left, and that Nelios was addressing her once again. 'Sorry, what?'

'I said this is also the venue for the pre-launch party for Nelios XV this evening. I'm hosting various ministers and industry people before the hotel officially opens next month. You will be added to the guest list.'

Surprise rifled through her. 'You want me to attend your party?'

He shrugged. 'Or you can stay in your bedroom and let the hours whittle away. Your choice.'

She shrugged. 'But… I don't have anything to wear.' She cringed at the feeble response. 'And I won't know anyone there.'

His gaze trailed over her once more, this time leaving incendiary fireworks where it touched her skin. 'That problem will be taken care of. And you'll be there as my guest. That's all that should matter.'

'I…okay.'

Something glinted in his eyes before they were veiled and he turned away. 'Find Andreas or Capaldi. They'll let you know if you can make yourself useful or where you can remain out of the way if not.'

She went looking for Capaldi because he was the less threatening of the two. So, of course, she immediately found Andreas surrounded by his staff as he fired off instructions. He stopped speaking and fixed her with a censorious stare when she approached. Firming her spine, she relayed Nelios's message.

Flint-grey eyes stared her down for a full minute before he called over a minion and conducted a low conversation. Then, relieving the woman of her tablet, he jerked his head for Vayle to follow to a dank office in the basement that looked like something out of the 1950s and held a desk, phone, a pad and pen.

He slapped down the tablet. 'These are the list of vendors we need to triple-check the supply status for the party. Call, confirm and bring me a list when you're done. And I wouldn't think of sabotaging it, if I were you.' With that statement coldly delivered, he started to walk away.

'I have a fair idea why you think you hate me. But can I ask that you at least give me the benefit of the doubt? I'll be out of your hair soon enough, but do you truly begrudge me fighting for my heritage and my family?'

He reversed direction and stopped six feet away. His whole body vibrated with the strength of his feeling. 'No child should be blamed for the circumstances of their birth. But the adults they grow up to be? Hell, yes, I'll hold them to the highest moral standard. You associating with Agnes Adamis even after learning what she and Apostolis did to Nelios is not painting yourself in glory. Especially since you're requesting the benefit of the doubt but are refusing to accommodate the possibility that the person with first-hand knowledge of what happened is giving you their first-hand experience.'

We share a dislike for wilful blindness. Nelios's words from last night made sense now.

'Do your work, Miss Lancaster,' he stated coldly, then left.

A little shakier than she wanted to admit, it took several minutes of wondering what the history between the two men was, and getting herself under control, before she was composed enough to pick up the phone.

And it took a further ten minutes to discover Andreas had given her 'busy' work, after several vendors expressed mild exasperation that they were being contacted for the umpteenth time. She ploughed through the list regardless, sometimes relying on sketchy Spanish to get her through a conversation. Three long hours later, she left the basement to deliver a list that Andreas promptly passed off to another minion before telling Vayle she was free to go.

Then she was shown into another overwhelmingly beautiful room overlooking acres of manicured garden. She stood at the window for a long minute before a ping from her phone had her dashing across the room.

It was another text from Agnes.

Happy to hear you're safe. But I still worry. Do what you need to do, then come home, agapite. Whatever happens, we'll survive. And while I know my Nelios will have his version of things, please, don't judge me too harshly. For good or ill, I had my reasons.

Just as before, the message triggered mixed emotions. And, just as before, when Vayle called back it went straight to voicemail. She wanted to respect that some issues were too important to discuss over the phone, but she couldn't shake the feeling that Nelios's bitterness might have fertile roots.

But until she knew the full truth...

She walked into the dressing room that dissected the bedroom from the bathroom, then stopped, her eyes widening at the clothes rail sitting next to the shopping bag containing her meagre clothes. Reminded that Nelios had said her party attire would be taken care of, she tentatively approached. The garment bags revealed three stunning party dresses complete with multiple accessories in jade-green, classic black and a blush-pink bohemian dress she never would've imagined choosing for herself. Yet her eye kept returning to the off-shoulder design, the bold cut-out pattern above the hip on the left side reminding her of the charged moment last night when Nelios had helped her with her zip.

* * *

Was that why she chose the dress? No. *Absolutely not.* Yet she couldn't suppress the low blanket of heat that suffused her all through the lunch that was delivered and eaten on her terrace as she watched final, feverish preparations for the party. And when she showered, blow-dried and styled her hair, then donned the pink gown, studded Valentino heels and delicate jewellery, before heading downstairs.

Nelios stood with Andreas and Capaldi in the large marble foyer decked out in red carpeting that unfurled outside to the pillared portico to welcome guests.

Fluttering butterflies in her belly turned to ravenous eagles when three sets of eyes turned her way, conversation freezing as she paused three steps from the bottom, her fingers clinging to the banister for dear life. They stared, then Andreas muttered something under his breath that had Nelios spearing him with a narrow-eyed look before, after responding sharply, he strode towards her. Andreas stormed off while Capaldi looked faintly bemused. A second later, he too walked away.

Which left her with Nelios, clean-shaven and impossibly handsome, unyieldingly imposing and mesmerising in a black dinner-jacket and snow-white studded shirt. He stopped before her and, despite her slight height advantage, Vayle didn't even fool herself into thinking she held an advantage.

Because it turned out having Nelios looking up at her held its own alarming thrill. Made her want to do foolish things, such as slide her arms over those muscle-packed shoulders, brush her fingers against the thick hair curling around his nape and press her lips to…

No.

Thorough and ferocious, his gaze trailed over, heightening that simmer in her belly. 'Your choice of wardrobe was adequate?' he enquired, but somehow Vayle believed he was simply making conversation; that his mind, like hers, was wholly preoccupied with the electric insanity seething beneath the surface.

'It was more than adequate. Thank you.'

'It's nothing,' he muttered roughly, eyes the colour of rich coffee lingering at that cut-out at her waist, on her hips.

'It's not nothing,' she parried softly. 'And I really appreciate it.'

That drew his attention to her face. To the pulse leaping at her throat. His nostrils flared for the briefest moment, then he stepped back. 'Then show that appreciation. Come.'

On shaky legs that had nothing to do with the four-inch heels she wore, she stepped down, then walked by his side to the front door...where photographers and reporters waited.

She blinked in surprise at the first flash, then the flurry that followed. It wasn't until Nelios was a few minutes into the interview, while she lingered one step behind him, that it occurred to her she was being used. That, while she'd seemingly blagged her way into having more time to state her case, he intended to take advantage of that time, as he'd openly warned her. Or it was something as simple and retributive as payback for the inconvenience she'd caused him?

Smarting a little at the idea, she started to step away, only to feel his strong arm slide around her waist.

'The most important guest is here. Be so kind as to not cause any disruption now, Vayle,' he rasped silkily without looking her way.

She stilled, her senses leaping with heady abandon when his hand brushed her bare skin.

'Petralis. A pleasure as always.'

Vayle forced herself to focus and gulped. She was face-to-face with Cabral Soares, one of the wealthiest men in the world. As if one billionaire tycoon wasn't overwhelming enough.

'Just between us, I'd been hoping you would build one of your famous hotels in my beloved city. I'm glad you weathered the red-tape storm to bring it to fruition.'

'So am I,' Nelios replied.

Cabral smiled at the stunningly dressed woman on his arm who dripped in diamonds. 'Marika and I are on the maiden Nelios Club Experience. We look forward to being surprised.'

Nelios's smile brimmed with self-assuredness. 'If it falls short in any way, let me know, but I don't think it will.'

'Confident as always.' Cabral turned to Vayle. 'And who is this delightful creature?' He shook her hand, a charming smile curving his lips.

Nelios looked down at her, eyes still charged with wild electricity making the storm brewing inside her rage that little bit wilder. 'This is Vayle Lancaster,' he said simply, with no extras.

And that was how he introduced her to many outrageously influential guests, all eager to pay homage to the powerful Nelios Petralis and the wonder and prestige he'd brought to their city: *Vayle Lancaster*. Letting them draw their own conclusions as to who she truly was or what her presence in his life meant.

And slowly a different kind of storm eddied to life in her chest. A storm fuelled by quiet outrage, three glasses of vintage champagne and, astonishingly, *hurt*. Because she was left in no doubt at all that Nelios had played her like a Stradivarius.

'This wasn't simply a benign invitation, was it?' she asked when, hours later, the last straggling guests had been firmly guided out by Capaldi and his retinue, and she found herself alone with Nelios.

The sight of him loosening his bow-tie to dangle down his chest, and tugging the studs of his shirt apart, threatened to derail her senses, but she rallied like never before.

'Benign?' he echoed without inflexion but his eyes remained watchful, complex with seething emotions held tightly under wraps. 'I can't say I've ever had that label bestowed on me, *glikia mou*.'

He drew to a stop before her and she came face-to-face with the strong column of his throat and his tanned, lightly hair-dusted chest. Her mouth dried. Her body positively vibrated with a need she could scarcely fathom, threatening once again to derail her outrage. She clawed it back with vicious purpose, using the fuel of it to suppress the uninhibited hunger he engendered in her with seemingly very little effort. 'You really don't care who you hurt, do you?'

'Tell me how you believe you've been hurt,' he invited, all loose-limbed sardonicism, a mogul replete after a successful evening of having people hang onto his every word.

'Stop it! You know exactly what you're doing. Those pictures outside, introducing me to the great and powerful without telling them my reason for being here.... Of course, it won't do to publicise the fact that you're in the middle of destroying my family name and the people I hold dear, will it?' She emphasised that last bit to draw a reaction, and predictably his jaw rippled with displeasure, his sensual lips thinning. 'You want Agnes to see, don't you? To open the newspapers in a few hours and see me standing next to you, looking like your...'

'Like my what, Vayle?' he encouraged with a dark rumble.

'Like your conquest!'

'Yes,' he bit out coldly. 'She doesn't deserve to have what she wants—to live happily into her dotage, having achieved her life's work. Not after what she and her husband did to me. You want to save her? I'll double what I'm offering for your hotel. But you will fire her, effective immediately. That's my condition. What you choose to do with your money is up to you. Save her with the proceeds of your hotel, if you wish; that's your prerogative. And, to sweeten the deal, I'll give you the pick of a marketing job in the Nelios hotel of your choosing, anywhere in the world. But you and you alone will work for me. Not her.'

Her eyes widened. As a sweetener, it was right up there in dream-come-true-land. Except she would betray Tolis's memory and hurt Agnes, while losing her inheritance to boot: the very definition of being caught between heaven and hell. 'That's…'

'Cruel?' A macabre twist of emotion turned his face into an abstract painting. 'It's far, far less than she deserves.'

'No, Nelios. My answer is no. I won't throw someone I love under the bus. Not for all the money in the world.'

His face shuttered, his eyes turning obsidian with cold fury and seething recrimination. 'Then there's nothing more to say. Your hotel will be mine, and I'll do with it what I please.' He turned and walked away.

And she stood there, locked in indignation and disbelief. Far too many minutes later, realising she couldn't let him get away with it, she chased after him, past waiting staff who watched her with varying expressions of interest which she blatantly ignored.

He was clearing the first-floor staircase and turning right, presumably towards his suite, when she scrambled up after him. And he was almost at a set of double doors when she shot past him and faced him, perhaps with more bravado than sense, stopping him in his tracks. Every inch of his grim expression warned her not to engage further. Not to attempt to traverse the impassable landscape of his glorious discontent. But chances had come and gone, and been under-utilised. It was finally now or never.

'You do realise this paints you with the same label, don't you? Because what you're suggesting is monstrous.'

A veritable cocktail of emotions swirled across his face before it settled into a rigid, savage mask. 'No, *glykia mou*. This makes me shockingly human, seeking to right a heinous wrong.' A spasm of anger ripped through the mask before he stifled it. 'I might be too late for one, but I will seek accountability for the other who's gone far too long without it.'

'God, you can barely even bring yourself to say her name, can you?'

'Why should I?' he said with a perfectly arctic tone. 'In a right and just world she would be *mama*,' he ground out, his chest rising and falling once, as if that was the only vulnerability he intended to allow himself, when an ocean of emotion seethed just beneath his surface. 'Now? Now she deserves nothing.'

He went to move past her. Where Vayle found the strength to step squarely into his path, she would never know.

'Take heed and stop,' he advised. His voice was even and yet it sounded like a charged echo left behind after a vicious eruption.

'Stop trying to make you feel? To make you see you're only hurting yourself in the long run by doing this? I won't. I can't.'

He tried to step back. She bunched her hand in his shirt,

gripping a handful of expensive cotton-silk blend. His breath hissed out.

'Vayle.'

'Nelios.'

They were captured, lashed together by emotions neither wanted to feel or define. A sound rumbled from him. Vayle heard a softer version slip from between her lips. His gaze dropped to her mouth. They parted as if commanded, her breathing turning sharper, shallower.

He changed direction, pressing into her hold. Her fist unclenched and splayed right over his heart, feeling the heavy *thud, thud, thud*, then feeling the beats gallop faster.

He pressed another inch closer and her fingers danced up past his breastbone, over his collar, sinking into the hair at his nape. They pulled him close, *closer*, held him captive again. Then she surged up on her tiptoes, her silent demand clear.

His mouth swooped onto hers. And what felt like a lifetime in the making was born of fire, of need, of desperate desire. His hands seized her waist and Vayle was only too glad to leap into his arms, wrapping her legs around his hips, delighting in his immediate lunge forward to throw open his suite door, stride inside and kick it shut.

She revelled in his large hands clasping her bottom, dragging her closer still until the imprint of his shaft was unmistakable. The hot groan that rumbled from his chest was smashed between their lips, right before his tongue breached her mouth, seeking entry she was only too giddy to provide.

And then he introduced her to a sensual plane so erotically sublime, she moaned helplessly. Then carried on moaning as he dropped her in the middle of his bed and shrugged off his jacket with jerky, near-desperate movements. 'Is this what you want?'

'Yes,' she breathed, because perhaps on some level she truly believed that it might be a way to reach him. Or, on a purely selfish, needy level, this feeling of having had her world torn from under her would always lead to this: to taking a small triumph from the raging need in his eyes, the escalation of his breathing and, yes, the bold imprint of his cock against his trousers, the culmination of his need for her.

'Yes,' she echoed, stronger, rising to her elbows so as not to miss a second of watching him bare his beautiful body to her.

And then Nelios Petralis was naked, a bronze god who she knew would ignite her every fantasy from now until eternity. But even the thought of him having that supreme power over her didn't matter in this moment. Not when her nipples screamed for attention and her core ached with the need for his possession.

Their eyes connecting, he reached for the side of her dress and, this time, Vayle did not stop her gasp when his fingers deliberately traced the outline of her exposed skin through the cut-out.

'This has been driving me insane all evening,' he said with that dark rumble that stated they might be engaging in a mutually desired connection, but the undercurrents still remained.

'Then do something about it,' she whispered huskily.

Eyes glinting with a feral light that set another raft of shivers dancing over her, Nelios gripped the delicate garment and tore it off her body.

Vayle didn't care. She'd planned to leave these possessions behind when she left tomorrow. When he treated her undergarments to the same vicious, sexy treatment, she gloried in it. And, when he proceeded to explore her with hands, teeth and mouth, drawing not one but two orgasms from her needy body before thrusting hard inside her with a muted shout, she threw herself into the act with an enthusiasm bordering on zealous abandon.

He didn't need to know that this was only her second time having sex; that the reactions he drew from her would be forever sealed in her memory as the transcendent experience it was. Nelios Petralis already had far too much power over her and those she cared about. But she was well aware that she drew equal zeal from him, if not feral desire, in those stolen hours of the night.

And, yes, she intended to hold that tiny win close to her chest, a bolster she suspected she would need in the coming weeks and months. Because, as much as it hurt her to admit it, when it came to salvaging her inheritance from the clutches of the ruthless billionaire, she'd failed.

CHAPTER FIVE

One year later

VAYLE DIDN'T WANT to be reminded of the complexities of human emotion as she stepped out of the lift on the third floor of her apartment building and approached her front door.

And yet, as she pushed the buggy bearing her three-month-old son along the brightly lit corridor, she was assailed by both joy and the overwhelming weight of heartache twisting round memories of the happiest day of her life. Even the tumult and wonder of the days, weeks and months that had preceded the day she'd given birth. Memories of feeling her baby kick for the first time, wondering if she had what it took to be a good enough parent when her father had failed her so badly.

Then, when the very thought of ever giving up on her own child had sent a surge of horror and rejection through her, she'd clung to that bolstering knowledge that she would never allow the trauma she'd suffered to be repeated on her baby. She'd built on that until nothing but pure love existed in her heart for the child she'd never expected to bear but loved beyond all reason even before he'd come into the world.

Her gaze dropped to the swaddled, sleeping occupant and her mouth predictably curved upward, joy superseding every other emotion for a long, heady moment as she basked in the pride and joy of motherhood. Of how her whole world now centred around one tiny human: Evangelos Nelios Petralis. The child she'd created with Nelios in a moment of wild insanity she still couldn't believe she'd been capable of.

The smile stayed in place until she reached her front door, then she took a deep breath. Because beyond it lay the kind of desolation that crept ever closer, like a fog over icy moors. Unbearable. All-encompassing. Unrelenting.

Agnes was deeply miserable. It wasn't until Vayle's return from Buenos Aires that the full scope of Agnes's hope had revealed itself. While Agnes might have tried dissuading her from going in the first place, Vayle had discovered that her surrogate mother had secretly hoped Vayle would succeed in reaching the son who was so determined to remain estranged from his mother. They'd finally spoken as Vayle had made her way back from Buenos Aires the morning after her night with Nelios. And, like a series of evil tumbling dominoes, nothing and no one had been able to halt what came next.

Nelios had succeeded in wresting the hotel from them. They'd been served with an eviction notice mere weeks later, after an unseemly large sum of money had been dumped in Vayle's bank account in payment. Then had come the worst insult. She'd discovered both she and Agnes had been blacklisted from every hospitality job worth having in London and beyond. It was then that Agnes had truly spiralled into despair, her every frantic effort to contact her son hitting a formidable brick wall.

It didn't matter to Vayle that she'd been unable to find

another job, or that she resented Nelios every time she was forced to use the money he'd paid her for Vayle Hotel. It didn't even matter that she'd then been secretly relieved that she had that money to fall back on when she'd discovered she was pregnant with Angelos. What wrenched at her heart, and continued to deeply hurt her, was how Agnes was suffering. How nothing Vayle did could coax her out of her anguish.

Vayle stopped for a moment to blink back tears and compose herself, her fingers tightening around the buggy's handle to bolster herself so she could be strong for Agnes.

On Vayle's return from Buenos Aires, Agnes had elaborated a little bit more, although Vayle sensed she'd still held something back from the story—something that made Agnes's eyes dim in deeper despair. She'd confirmed that they'd had to leave Nelios in the care of Tolis's friend to take the much-needed job with George Lancaster because, yes, he had strictly forbidden them to bring a child to the premises of his precious hotel.

She'd accepted Agnes's tearful insistence that the situation had only been meant to be very temporary; that they'd explained that to Nelios, and that she and Tolis had tried their hardest to find their son after he'd run away from his foster home. And, after Vayle's own shocking discovery that she was pregnant in the weeks following her escapade in Buenos Aires, she'd found herself experiencing a sliver of Agnes's anguish.

Because she'd borne Nelios Petralis an heir he'd never bothered to acknowledge...

Quelling emotions that threatened to unravel every time she thought of that night with Nelios, and the pitiless events that had followed the next morning, she re-pinned the smile on her face and entered the flat. Agnes glanced up from the living room sofa, bleary eyed and looking way over her sixty-three years, the ghost of a smile drifting over her face before it fell on Angelos. Then, in a belly-hollowing replication of her son's features, a complex series of emotions drifted over her face: joy; sorrow; anguish; pride.

'I brought you some food from the Greek café you like,' Vayle ventured once she'd shut the door behind her.

She wasn't surprised when the predictable head shake came, followed by the soft, 'You have it, *glikia mou*. I'm not hungry.'

Vayle heart lurched at the endearment she recalled being uttered in a much deeper voice.

'How is *agapoula mou*?' she asked, cutting through Vayle's impending plea for her to eat something.

'Sleeping like an angel,' she replied with quiet pride. She'd been blessed with a no-fuss baby who knew what he wanted and, as long as he received it, was very content.

'His father was the same.' Agnes's voice caught and Vayle's heart squeezed when tears brimmed the older woman's lashes. Abandoning the carton of moussaka she'd meant to coax Agnes with, she crossed the room and pressed a tissue into her hand. She'd barely swiped at her eyes before they fixed on Vayle.

The vice tightened, as she sensed what was coming. What Agnes had insisted she do with varying degrees of persistence.

'Did you try again?' the older woman asked.

Vayle swallowed a mixture of concern, indignation and frustration. Now she had Angelos, Vayle couldn't fathom how Agnes and Tolis had gone over two decades without tearing the world apart to find their son. But what she did understand, and fully empathised with, was that some things were simply out of one's control. So she took a sustaining breath and exhaled. 'I told you. It's not that simple.' She knew. She'd tried several times to reach Nelios and had met a very formidable wall every time. A wall that had finally threatened dire consequences if she persisted. 'He doesn't want to know,' she added, ignoring the rough squeeze in her chest.

Since Vayle knew first-hand how it felt to slam her head against the brick wall of Nelios Petralis's fortress, she'd recognised quickly that retreat was her best option. Even if it meant withstanding Agnes's palpable sorrow as her gaze shifted to rest on Angelos. Rising, Agnes walked over to the buggy and stared down with fond sadness at her grandson before brushing her fingers down his cheek. When she returned to her seat, her air of despair was so thick, it clogged Vayle's throat.

Eventually, when at Vayle's urging the older woman went to lie down, Vayle snatched up her phone, giving in to the urge to look up Nelios yet again. He wasn't exactly unavoidable, but she'd weaned herself off her near-obsessive cyber-stalking the day of her first scan.

And she'd *mostly* succeeded, damn it. So what if his Buenos Aires launch of Nelios XV had been hailed as the most successful in recent history? Or that the hotel had featured in every architectural, hotel and property magazine for months? Or that Nelios himself had graced the covers of *Time*, *People* and *Forbes* as the most influential genius on earth?

Or that every image of him had sent a mini-shockwave through her? Had made her achingly aware of her near-zealous interest when her eyes had burned because she'd stared unblinkingly at him?

She couldn't forget he'd had her unceremoniously thrown

out of his mansion the morning after he'd put his seed inside her. Or, worse, what he'd done after *that*...

But for Agnes's sake... Her fingers hovered briefly over her phone before they moved of their own volition, typing his name into the search engine. And there he was—collecting yet another accolade. Her breath caught. *He was right here in London.* Then Vayle's eyes shifted...to the woman on his arm...and her heart lurched, wild and unhinged.

She blinked and shook her head. It was unthinkable—laughable, even. Twin sparks of inexplicable anger and bemusement ignited in her belly. Because the woman... could've been Vayle's sister. The thought that Nelios was dating a woman who looked like her made her insides jump because... Had she made that much of an impact on him?

Another choking sensation rose: *jealousy; anger.*
No. Focus. This is about Agnes—only *Agnes.*

But the spikes of turbulent emotion wouldn't dissipate. So, without stopping to think, she scrolled through to the number she'd called a year ago, far too many times before she'd wised up, and pressed the button.

It rang long enough for her insides to churn. For the voice to demand what the hell she was doing.

'Miss Lancaster, I thought we agreed that—'

'I don't care what you think, Andreas. I have a message for Nelios—and, yes, I know you're with him right now. Tell him I thought him many things, but a coward wasn't one of them. Or maybe all that tough posturing was just an act. Tell me, do you feed off each other's trauma to justify the way you treat others, or it is just him?'

He inhaled sharply. 'What did you just say?'

'He really should've got me to sign one of those NDA thingies. But, since he didn't, and he's made damn sure

I'm blacklisted anyway, I'm thinking of going on a revenge tour. Who knows? Maybe I'll bring his mother with me and hang out all his dirty laundry for the world to see.' She grimaced, her fingers tightening around the phone as she cringed inside. Was she taking this too far?

'What the hell do you want?'

For him to acknowledge his son! Thankfully, she kept that wish unspoken. She'd tried for Angelos's sake until she'd drawn the line at placing her precious son in the line of fire for rejection.

'I want him to meet with his mother for one hour. Tomorrow.'

Thick, furious silence greeted her demand. Then the line went dead.

Her breath whooshed out and, as she wilted into the sofa, Vayle had the disturbing inkling that she might've done the very thing she'd accused Nelios of—Hulk-smashing when a delicate touch was needed.

Should she call back—apologise? Maybe…

She jumped when a text pinged. Eyes wide, she read the message.

5pm tomorrow. Nelios VIII London. NXL Suite.

For the second time in as many minutes, her breath exploded out of her lungs. She'd poked the beast. And it had finally responded.

Whether it would end up devouring them both was another matter. She tossed her phone away, rose and for the next hour busied herself so she wouldn't dwell on what the following twenty-four hours would entail. Hell, Nelios hadn't even stated whether he wanted her there or if he wanted to see just his mother.

Why would he want you? He's already got your lookalike.

The reminder sent shards of glass through her belly, robbing her of breath and calmness. Because this level of distress made her feel suspiciously as if *she cared*.

And she *absolutely* did not...

The sound of the doorbell brought both relief and mild exasperation, the freedom from her unwanted thoughts warring with not wanting Angelos to be woken up just yet.

Rushing to the door, she opened it. And froze at the sight of the man poised in the doorway, conjured up from recklessness into real life, looking from head to toe like the Greek statue of his homeland.

'Nelios! W-what are you doing here? You said tomorrow!'

Dark-brown eyes fixed on her for an age without responding, then conducted a searing head-to-toe scrutiny, reminding her that she hadn't brushed her hair since morning. That she, in her jeans and simple top, was no match for the designer-gowned woman clinging to his arm in that photo.

Vayle watched him contain every expression that threatened to escape until his face was a rigid mask. After what felt like an aeon later, after every atom in her body was singing a frenzied aria and his eyes were near molten, he glanced into the flat.

'Where is she?'

'She's resting. And you didn't answer me. What are you doing here?'

'Did you not summon me, or were your threats as empty as the lies you're still being spoon-fed?'

'I...yes, okay, I may have laid it on a little thick to Andreas, but I wanted to get your attention.'

His head tilted. 'Well, now you have it,' he said smoothly,

low and deadly. 'Do you not know what to do with me now you have me, Vayle?'

She licked her lips, the connotations making her thighs clench, her nipples hard. Crossing her arms to hide his visceral effect on her, she shrugged. 'This isn't about me. It's about your mother. And, if I knew you could be summoned so easily, I would've done it ages ago.'

His gaze swung to her then, almost taken aback by her forced, glib tone. She would've smiled but, far from hoping she would be spared this time from the effect of the electric forcefield Nelios carried with him wherever he went, Vayle discovered she was very much caught in the sizzling static.

'For someone treading on dangerous ground, you don't seem too worried,' he rasped, his eyes still boring daggers into her.

She shrugged. 'I know what it's like to be caught in an emotional wind tunnel, when all around you is a force-five tornado, so no, I'm not worried. I am perfectly fine right now. Happy, even, despite these circumstances,' she tossed out because far be it for him to think she was still fixated on the humiliation of the morning after their night before. 'So, yes, I can be sceptical as to whether anyone on earth has the power to summon you anywhere without a little...incentive.'

'Believe me, you have no idea what I'm feeling right now.'

'Okay, feel free to share it, then,' she invited softly.

He opened his mouth, then seemed to change his mind. He looked around, as if to remind himself of why he'd come. A detached kind of bleakness descended over his face and this time the expression wasn't quickly dispatched.

'You could've waited till tomorrow. Why the rush?' Her heart thumped, hoping. She knew what she wanted, at least where he and Agnes were concerned. Beyond that...no, she wasn't going to think about her son who slept out of sight in his portable cot. It was a waste of time. Nelios hadn't come here for him. 'Because if you've come not to talk to Agnes, but to cause further injury to her, then—'

'Cause injury—?' He cut himself off in near wonder. 'What about the injury *she* caused *me*?' he seethed. But again, it wasn't just fury rolling across his face. It was deep, ingrained anguish, like a wound, buried deep and newly ripped wide open.

'If it's retribution you're looking for, isn't what you've already done enough? You took away your own mother's purpose by blacklisting her. And I won't even start on how you stabbed me in the back as well. What did I ever do to you, Nelios?' Her breath hitched a tiny bit and she hated herself, and him, for it.

His eyes raked her face, once, twice. And, heaven help her hopelessness, but she thought she saw him lose a shade of colour, maybe even experience a flash of remorse, before his expression froze into neutrality again.

'Where is my... Where is she?' he repeated through barely moving lips.

'I told you, she's resting. If you'd bothered to tell me you'd changed the time...'

A shadow crossed his face. 'Andreas responded without my input. I prefer to face some threats head-on, even empty ones.'

Her mouth twisted in a mockery of a smile that seemed to have a direct link to the vice around her heart. 'Some?' she echoed, hating herself for thinking about how he'd left her sleeping in his bed without even the courtesy of a goodbye.

Was it her imagination or had he winced just then? She

hoped he had. That he had other emotions over and above the vengeance locked in his heart for the mother who'd brought him into the world. Over and above the wild desire he'd let loose that night in Buenos Aires, followed by the sheer cruelty he'd displayed the morning after.

'Don't test me,' he warned far too coolly.

'Or what? Haven't you already done your worst to me, Nelios?'

He stiffened. And just like that every last emotion was stripped from his face, leaving a cold mask with glinting eyes. 'Don't presume you know what I'm fully capable of, *glikia mou*—'

'Don't call me that,' she snapped before she could stop herself. 'I'm not your sweet anything.'

His nostrils flared but his expression didn't change. '*Ne*, you're right. You're not.' His dismissive gaze landed on the two doors down the short hallway. 'This is the only time I can spare. Or I walk out the door and any more of her incessant attempts to hound me will be treated as harassment.'

Her mouth gaped. 'Agnes is still reaching out to you?' Vayle had believed she'd stopped after Nelios's stony silence.

His eyes turned flint-hard. 'I see she's still keeping things from you.'

She snapped her mouth shut. 'Don't start. Or I'll…'

One eyebrow arched. 'Or you'll what?'

She pursed her lips, knowing there were no further threats to make.

'A word of advice, Vayle. Get your head out of the sand before it's too late. Or you will—'

The small cry interrupted his unwelcome advice. His gaze darted around the room, surprise dousing his face.

The cry came again, and his sharp eyes captured hers. 'What is that?'

Her heart leapt into her throat, but she fought the apprehension wrapping around her whole being. '*That* is exactly what it sounds like.'

At some point in the future, Vayle would wonder what would've happened if Angelos hadn't chosen then to wake up. If he'd continued sleeping, blissfully unaware of the tumult unfolding just feet away. But he hadn't. And, now he'd decided it was time to remind the world—and his father—that he existed, nothing was going to stop him. The cry hitched to a stop for a handful of seconds, no doubt to give his mother the chance to do the right thing and shower his presence with endless adoration.

She went into the bedroom she shared with him, just as he decided her time was up. His impatient cry filled the room, quickening her last few steps. She was intensely aware that Nelios had followed close behind her. That she hadn't answered his question and he meant to pry a response from her.

'It's okay, darling. I'm here. Shhh, no need to make such a ruckus,' she crooned lovingly.

Then, the precious bundle in her arms and her heart in her throat, Vayle turned to where a statue-still Nelios stood frozen. Despite not moving, he occupied every square inch of the doorway until she couldn't breathe, couldn't think, couldn't see anything else but him. Or that convoluted parade of emotions which included shock, bewilderment and now, incredibly...*jealousy*?

She didn't understand why his gaze darted towards where her left hand was tangled in the blanket. And, when it searched and apparently didn't discover what he was looking for, recaptured her gaze. 'You're married?'

Why was his voice so hoarse? So *accusatory*?

'You may have turned my life inside out a year ago, but I don't believe I owe you any information now,' she replied tartly.

Angelos whimpered, perhaps sensing the tension in the air. Or perhaps it was simply a demand for milk now he was awake. She shifted him in her arms, and again Nelios's gaze darted to her left hand. She realised he was looking for a ring, and almost laughed.

'It's the twenty-first century, Nelios. A woman isn't doomed to ruin simply because she has a child out of wedlock.' Her inner hysteria threatened to spill over at the very thought of dating another man while pregnant and then going as far as to marry said mystery man—amidst the turbulence of having Nelios proceed with his plans to rip Vayle Hotel from her grasp, leaving them homeless and having to scramble to rearrange their lives. She would've needed to be Wonder Woman herself. And, while she was proud of herself for battling through the trials and tribulations of the past year, she was well-versed in what it felt like to approach breaking point. To teeter over the very edge of the abyss and force herself back just in time.

Another wave of shock travelled through him. 'So the child is yours?' he pressed a little jaggedly.

This time she frowned. 'What are you talking about? Of course he is.'

She didn't think it possible but he seemed to harden further, his breath locked in his towering body. Frantic eyes fell on Angelos, his gaze sharpening into probing drills. Whatever he saw made the great Nelios Petralis positively *stagger* for the first time since she'd known him.

Perhaps it was the brown eyes her baby had inherited from him, or the tiniest hint of a dimple in his chin that would grow as prominent as his father's one day. Or maybe it was an elemental feeling of recognition between father and son she wasn't privy to. Angelos fell silent then beneath his father's scrutiny, his wide eyes taking in the man who looked as though he was fighting a great inner battle. Whether he won or not was questionable because, when he next spoke, his voice remained gravel-rough.

'I am going to ask you a question, Vayle. And I would be extremely appreciative if you didn't play games with me.'

'I don't—'

'How old is this child?' he cut across her, his voice no longer shaken but scalpel-sharp.

Now, Vayle froze. 'What? You know how old he is. He's exactly three months next week. Why would you—?'

'Vayle.' His chest rose, held, fell, eyes turned midnight dark, pinning her in place. 'Is this child... Is he mine?'

The cycle of outrage at the question came and went in split seconds because it occurred to her that she'd missed something—several 'somethings', as it turned out. Nelios Petralis wasn't dim, far from it. He was the most astute man she knew. Yet, every sign pointed to him being in pitch darkness about his son's existence. How was that even possible?

She stared down at her baby, the most precious thing in her life and felt something seismic move through her. A warning? A rallying cry?

Against what? Surely he wouldn't...

Another bedroom door opened behind her, but the brief reprieve she yearned for to parse through what was happening never came because Agnes stepped out and immediately froze at the sight of her son.

'Demetrius.'

'That is no longer my name,' Nelios growled, a mighty

predator swinging his mighty paws. 'If you respect nothing else, respect that,' he said through gritted teeth.

She went sheet-white, and stumbled back against the door.

Nelios lunged towards her—so he wasn't entirely unfeeling after all—but Agnes straightened before he reached her and he froze halfway between Vayle and his mother.

And there, caught in some invisible vortex, his head swung from his mother to her. 'It's now clear one of you orchestrated this. So I will ask again—is this child mine?' he breathed.

She might have crafted things into being for Agnes's sake, but Vayle resented the unfounded accusation. Her temper flared anew.

'How dare you come here, all superior and indignant, asking questions you already know the answers to? You claim to despise games, which begs the question—what game are *you* playing? You might have ignored his existence up till now, but don't you dare pretend you didn't know you had a son!'

Nelios had never been in a war zone, beyond the one he'd been thrown into when he'd been too young and ill-equipped to withstand it. He'd never felt bullets whistle about his head though, sure, he knew only too well what the sound of flying fists felt like when they landed.

But in this moment, when emotional landmines exploded across his every sense, he knew what soldiers of war experienced. What it felt like to have one's life flash before one's eyes as devastation unravelled all around. For a long stretch of time, he saw everything he'd imagined the rest of his life would be detonate and turn to ash right before his eyes, leaving him with the most desolate landscape he'd yet endured. But, curiously, even that image didn't linger.

It attempted to morph, take a different shape. He shut it down before it solidified. Because screw fate for attempting to rearrange his destiny without his permission. Screw karma for this...*unacceptable* effort to show him a different landscape from the one he'd meticulously drawn out for himself while enduring those fists and darkness and humiliation.

Ignored his existence up till now...

Know you had a son...

He shook his head, wondering for a moment, but knowing he hadn't misheard her. Vayle Lancaster had many faults but she'd never tossed out words she didn't find a way of expressing one way or another.

Especially the *one particular way* that still had the power to turn his insides out, which he most definitely wasn't going to think about. Even if the consequences of it was right there in his face, in the form of a cherubic angel staring at him with open curiosity an infant this young surely shouldn't possess. Unless that infant was *his* and thus superior in all the ways that counted.

His child.

The ominous sensation that had taken hold of him when he'd first set eyes on the boy built now, seizing every corner of his being. Setting off a pendulum of emotions he only seemed to feel around Vayle Lancaster.

No, that wasn't true. Unbelievably, the woman quietly sobbing behind him also held that power, even after all this time. It was almost laughable that, having sworn never to clasp eyes on these two people again in this lifetime, he now found himself caught in the maelstrom of emotions they both triggered in him.

Well, *three* now. He didn't doubt that, had Apostolis been alive, he too would've merrily riled him. His heart lurched at the thought of the father he'd never seen again after that fateful night. The father who'd thrown him away.

Looking into the child's eyes, something tight, profound and earth-shaking seized his chest, convulsed, jump-started and changed the very fibre of his being.

Glad you didn't have that vasectomy now?

His breath caught, unprepared for that hissing taunt. For the unguarded punch to his solar plexus at the notion that this child, who had the power to trigger such weighty emotions in him, might never have existed.

Which meant what, exactly?

He shook his head again and redoubled his effort to corral his control. And when he succeeded—because he *always* succeeded—he levelled his most fearsome glare at the woman holding the child…*his son*…in her arms.

'I'm willing to accommodate your belief that I knew about my…about this baby's existence.' *Son.* Something inside him veritably *rumbled* at uttering the word he'd stumbled on. He, who *never, ever* stumbled. But Nelios knew, and readily accepted, that the moment he took full possession of the truth a great many things would change, in ways even he wasn't prepared for. So, yes, he was well within his rights to buy himself a little time. 'Just as I hope you will accommodate my need to get to the bottom of it.'

Ne, he sounded more than reasonable. Surprising, considering the tsunami of sensations bombarding him. She must've thought so too, because those alluring blue eyes, eyes he'd watched glaze with pleasure so pure he'd never witnessed the likes of it before, widened a fraction.

'I…could see my way to doing that,' she murmured, then her gaze darted past him. 'What about Agnes?'

His teeth clenched and he forced himself to turn round. To face the woman who'd once held his hand on the way to school before she'd turned into a monster. 'What do you want? Why am I here?'

Agnes's lips quivered for a second. Her gaze lingered on his face before they dropped. 'I wanted to talk to you. Explain what really happened.' Her face twisted. 'And some other things I think you're old enough to know now.'

A different sort of juddering moved through him. 'New information?' he jeered. 'What could possibly explain anything away now?' Nelios unfurled fists he'd bunched without conscious thought. Somewhere at the back of his brain, the hissing voice sounded again, demanding to know who was sticking their head in the sand now. But he refused to heed that vexing question. The simple truth was that he was reaching saturation point—wasn't open to new stimuli.

He cut off the swell of bleakness attempting to drown him and spun round to face Vayle, and the baby, who turned his near-bald head to watch him with... *Thee mou,* was he getting judgement from his own son too?

Impossible.

'We need to talk, Vayle,' he said as evenly as the nonsensical tempest raging inside him would allow him. 'Away from here,' he added, just to be clear.

'But...' Whatever she'd been about to say withered away when her gaze jerked past him to Agnes. Whatever passed between the two of them—and, no, the reaction unfurling in his chest wasn't jealousy—her face softened with a sort of understanding and she nodded. 'Okay, I will spare you an hour. No more, just so we're clear.'

He did well to keep his furious rejection of that limitation to himself. He was experienced in life and business enough to know when to bide his time and bite his tongue until he gained the ground he needed.

And Nelios knew, as he cast one look at Agnes and then

at the woman who was settling his son into his push-chair in preparation to wheel it out, that far from coming here to slam shut the book of his horrendous past as he'd believed, a whole new chapter had unexpectedly opened up.

One he intended to have full control over.

No matter what.

'That look between you and Agnes. What was that about?' he asked the moment they stepped into the lift.

She lifted her gaze from the child, withdrew her stroking finger from his cheek and straightened. Then she shot him a glance that was all defiance and fire. 'It was a look that said we're in this thing together, no matter what. And, before you accuse me of soft feelings as if they're flaws I should be ashamed of, I really don't care what you think.'

Since it was exactly what he'd intended to say, he far from appreciated having the rug pulled from beneath his feet.

'Where are you going?' he asked when they reached the ground floor and she turned away from the main entrance.

'To my car. Where else?'

He examined the contraption his son reclined in. 'Is this one of those carriers that converts into a car seat?'

She nodded warily.

'Then we don't need to travel separately. I will have you delivered back here when we're done.'

His driver pulled up the moment they stepped outside. And if the older man was astonished by the novel sight of his boss escorting a woman and child to his car, he hid it skilfully, as he was paid handsomely to do, briskly picking up the skeleton of the buggy Vayle had collapsed while she expertly secured the portable seat in the spacious car.

'No Andreas tagging along?' she asked airily once she'd

slid into the seat and secured her seatbelt, but he noted the tight edge framing the enquiry.

'We're not joined at the hip, surprisingly.'

'No? You could've fooled me,' she shot back.

Nelios inspected her expression, something tightening inside him. 'What is that supposed to mean?' His best friend was assertive but he wouldn't overstep in any way that would put their relationship in jeopardy. He knew that as surely as he knew the lines dissecting his palm.

She shook her head. 'Nothing important,' she said, completely undermining her words.

He prudently chose to ignore it—for now. His eyes slid to the car seat. 'What is his name?' he asked, that roughness he couldn't clear away back in his voice.

She held in her response for a few long seconds. 'Evangelos Nelios Petralis. But I call him Angelos.'

Every atom of his being seemed to clench into stillness except his heart, which raced with an unfettered kind of recklessness he'd never felt before. Not even when he'd feared he was close to death in that alley the night his life had taken yet another course.

Theos. 'You named him after me?' A son she'd never meant to tell him about? He wasn't sure whether he should be furious or floored. Or, damn it, both!

'I'm not the kind of woman who believes a child should be punished for who or what their father turns out to be. He's yours. And mine. So I chose his name accordingly.'

The boy turned at his mother's voice, as if he recognised his name even this young. Then he gave a demanding cry.

'He's hungry. I need to feed him. How far away are we from wherever we're going?' she asked, offering the baby one finger to distract him. Which helped—temporarily, he suspected.

'Five minutes. Perhaps less,' he replied, then plunged into the first subject that niggled. 'We used protection.'

She shot him another of those fiery glares. 'Evidently not even the world's most powerful and influential man is safeguarded from faulty condoms.'

And it really was as irrefutable as that.

They arrived at Nelios VIII, and were whisked to his private residence within minutes. He watched her make a beeline for the living room sofa as soon as they entered, taking not a single interest in her luxurious surroundings.

Realising that she meant to breastfeed his son, Nelios was struck anew by the impending experience. Then by all the ones he'd missed up to now. Trailing behind them, he knew propriety dictated he should look away, give her privacy. But, hell, theirs had never been a remotely proper connection. She had literally dropped at his feet at their second meeting and things had gone increasingly insane from there. Why relabel it something else now? And, since she didn't seem remotely self-conscious about performing a very natural act...

His brain short-circuited when she loosened the belt of her wraparound dress, unclipped her nursing bra and positioned Angelos at her breast. His eager, hungry son wriggled, then latched on the moment he was able. Nelios realised his breath was locked in his throat with wonder, with a prowling kind of possessiveness. Then with a growing certainty that this would be the last time he missed a single thing about this boy. *His son.* So he eased back in his seat and propped his ankle on his knee, patient now that he'd allowed the reforming landscape to unfold. To show him what he already knew in his blood.

'What did you want to talk about?' she asked a little hesitantly, perhaps sensing the change in the air. The change in her very destiny.

'I had intended to talk about a great many things. But I've come to accept that, while what has come before matters, it isn't as vital as what comes next.'

A pulse visibly leapt in her throat then started to race in earnest. He curled his hand over his ankle when a different need struck: the need to reacquaint himself with the silky skin overlaying that pulse. To drift his tongue over that evidence of her life force and hear that throaty gasp he'd heard far too often in his dreams.

Nelios accepted that, all these months later, a peculiar kind of longing for her still remained. That perhaps he'd left that Buenos Aires bedroom too quickly. That Andreas musing as to Nelios's affinity for dating a certain type of woman since that night who were all poor carbon copies of the one sitting in front of him—women who were inevitably packed off before they even saw the inside of his bedroom—meant something important. Unfinished business that needed dealing with.

'And what exactly is that?'

He looked from mother to child and back again, a primitive claim that defied civility and reason taking full, complete control of him.

'That I want my son. And I will have him. And because you will put up all sorts of a fight—which I will win, by the way—the culmination of it all will be that you will marry me. As soon as possible. And we will raise our son together.'

CHAPTER SIX

SHE REFUSED. OF COURSE she did. And she argued—vigorously. Because…well, she had no choice.

A mere two weeks later, though, Vayle was sipping coffee just before noon on her wedding day, replaying that conversation, as she had so many times, and convincing herself she'd done the right thing for everyone involved.

Well, perhaps not for herself, if she was honest. But for those she cared about: Agnes and Angelos. They were the ones she'd fought for. On whose behalf she'd extracted those conditions from Nelios. Conditions which, in hindsight, it seemed he'd accepted with healthy opposition but surprisingly not as much vigour as she'd imagined. Which had then led her to wonder if she'd missed something in the small print of their agreement that would come back to bite her in the ass when she least expected it.

Taking another sip, she set the cup down on its saucer. As much as she wanted to finish it, she was jittery enough as it was. Hell, she'd been jittery ever since that day when Nelios had stated with unyielding steel while they'd been caught in that sensory force field, 'Make no mistake—I will have full access to my child, Vayle.'

Her hand had wrapped tighter around Angelos, happily

oblivious and ensconced in his milk-guzzling. 'I sense a very large "or else" in there.'

Her attempted fierce reply had wobbled a little at the end, but she'd kept her daring gaze on him. Because, yes, she was a mother bear, and she would fight to the death for her child.

'Or else I will fight you for custody,' he stated evenly. As if he hadn't been threatening to raze her world to the ground just as effectively as he'd snatched her hotel. As if he'd been picking out a colour scheme for one of his stunning hotels.

'Then I'll see you in court,' she'd replied just as coolly and that time, thankfully, her voice had held.

It had been *his* nostrils that flared. *His* ankle that had left his knee to plant on the floor, his long arms dangling between his knees as he'd speared her with his gaze. *His* jaw that had rippled the tiniest bit before he'd loosened it.

'You would put yourself through that?'

She'd stared at him, really stared. Then she'd asked the question throbbing across her brain. 'For the sake of clarity, I didn't lose my faculties during childbirth. So I know I'm not imagining all the times I called you and emailed you and even left a letter with your right-hand man—despite, I might add, you sending him to do your dirty work the morning after we had sex, to dispatch me like some used spare part you no longer needed. So why the hell are you acting as if you're the wronged party here?'

He'd turned to ice. 'Excuse me?'

Hurt, anger and humiliation trawled through her, reawakened by memories she'd desperately not wanted to relive. 'Which part do you want to be excused from, exactly? The part where you took off in your helicopter that morning without bothering to wake me? The part where you sent Andreas to make sure I wasn't around when you returned? Or where you instructed him to tell me never to attempt to grace your presence again because you were done with me?'

A hint of colour washed his cheeks and Vayle would've mistaken it for embarrassment on anyone else. Not on Nelios. Every move he made was with calculated precision and intent. It was why, after several attempts to contact him, she'd accepted that he truly meant to cut her off. That he wasn't interested in knowing the consequences of their night together.

'Andreas was supposed to put you on a plane back to England. Any embellishment made was on his own initiative. And your claim that you tried to contact me—'

'Are you calling me a liar, Nelios?' she butted in, keeping her voice low so Angelos, who stared raptly at her every expression, didn't pick up on her roiling emotions. 'And are you saying, had I decided to stay, you would've been ecstatic to see me on your return?' The fierce blaze, then the immediate shuttering of his gaze told her everything she needed to know. 'Do not attempt to rewrite history. It shames both of us.'

'Watch it, Vayle.'

'Another "or else"? Can we agree that I'm far from impressed by these deep-throated threats? So it's pointless to keep throwing them about. Sure, I know what horrors you're capable of. But I will defend my child until my last breath.'

Perhaps it was a trick of the light, but she thought he lost a shade of colour. 'Defend—from me?' he demanded through thinned lips. And for a moment she was almost convinced she'd wounded him somehow. But, like the great and mythical phoenix, he rose from that almost immediately. Stronger, more powerful, more visually, completely, *unfairly* arresting than ever. And, when he approached, her breath strangled then swiftly abandoned her lungs. He crouched before her, placing his hands on either side of her thighs on the sofa. His eyes lingered on her face for an age, then dropped to Angelos, where they stayed, *stayed* and *stayed*.

'I asked you a question,' he breathed softly without taking his eyes off his son. 'Do you believe I will deliberately harm my own flesh and blood?'

It was a weakening mistake to remember in that moment how he'd helped her when she'd developed her awful cramp. How he'd fed her on his plane and called off the authorities in Ascension. How he'd bought her a ticket home—certainly to aid her swift exit from his life—when he could easily have dumped her at the end of the street and left her to fend for herself. And today, when he'd reached out for his mother when she'd stumbled.

Nelios was ruthless, intransigent, driven and hell-bent on revenge against those he believed had wronged him. But was he ever unjustifiably wicked or unkind? Her jaw moved, but Vayle couldn't quite find the words to counter. So she settled for a middling, 'Maybe...maybe not.'

Censure filmed his eyes. 'Is that stubbornness or malice holding you back, *glikia mou*? A wish to hurt me the way you think I've hurt you?'

'I don't think it. I've lived it,' she confessed with a drowning rush of memory. He'd gifted her an unforgettable night, then had topped it with humiliation.

His eyelids swept down, veiling his expression as before. 'I am not entirely...convinced I couldn't have handled things differently,' he finally rasped.

Her eyes widened. 'An admission? My,' she said, then

wondered why she wasn't appeased. Why part of her yearned to beat his chest for every moment of humiliation she'd felt when Andreas had knocked on the suite door and calmly informed her she had half an hour to vacate the premises, on Nelios's orders—*if* she wanted the ticket for the flight leaving in less than two hours. He'd mocked her when she'd asked to speak to Nelios, informing her that, once the great Nelios Petralis was done with a woman, he never went back.

Especially a woman like her whom he shouldn't have touched in the first place.

Andreas hadn't said those final words, but it'd been vastly evident he meant them from his sneer and the tone of his voice.

Then she wondered if her disgruntlement had something to do with the woman she'd seen on Nelios's arm last night. She pushed *that* away.

'Do you know what it felt like to do the literal walk of shame?' she asked bitterly. 'What am I talking about? Of course you don't. Men like you think you rule the world and everyone in it, don't you? Well, you don't own me.' She enunciated clearly so there would be no ambiguity.

Of course that temporary ebbing of his haughtiness reversed, his strong jaw jutting until he was staring down the blade of his aquiline nose. 'I don't wish to own you. But even I recognise that you and my son come as a package deal. Hence my offer. Marry me, and there will be no need for unnecessary acrimony.' His lips twisted. 'I'm even open to us parting ways…eventually. With certain conditions in place, of course.'

Ice-cold, a little thrown by that, and caught in warped bemusement, she asked, 'And what would those be?'

'That we remain married until Angelos is of age—

eighteen years at the minimum. That under no circumstances are you to disappear from his life unless those circumstances are out of your control or with meticulous advance planning that will not leave him emotionally scarred.' His eyes turned to merciless flint then, the unvarnished evidence of him reliving his own past right there in his eyes. 'Agree to that and I will concede to a demand or two.'

Her brows lifted. Perhaps she should've stopped the words that spilled out but this was…a lot. And no one had said she was barred from reeling or reacting with some sassiness of her own. 'Just *one or two* in return for eighteen years of my life? What a hard bargain you drive. Go on, then, dazzle me with these concessions.'

'Ten million dollars on our wedding day. A further three million for every year we stay married. Plus any marketing position you want in my empire.'

'All out of the goodness of your heart?' she taunted, still attempting to drive him into betraying an emotion. To scratch beneath his icy facade.

He shrugged. 'Why not? Besides, I don't want the sleazy media accusing me of taking advantage of you.'

'Did you care about how you would be perceived when you took away my livelihood?' she challenged.

'You mean when I left you several hundred thousand pounds richer?' he parried.

She tugged her baby closer. 'Money isn't everything.'

'Neither is clinging to an outdated monstrosity that was worth nothing, certainly nowhere near what I paid for it. Tell me honestly—before I solved your problem for you and paid way over the market price, when was the last time you'd seen a decent profit? And don't trot out the "money isn't everything" excuse. Bursary or not, you didn't go through university and come out with two degrees to manage a failing business whose only appeal was that it bore your name. A business which fell apart at the slightest pressure from competition.'

'Slightest pressure?' she scoffed. 'You're joking, right? You ruthlessly targeted us and didn't let up until we had no choice but to give in.'

His hand slashed through the air. 'And you're well aware of my primary reasons for that. But we're straying from the subject. You can be my opponent in the custody court or my wife. You decide.'

The final, clanging ultimatum.

She sucked in a slow breath. Despite single mothers having been a thing since the dawn of time, she knew firsthand the judgement that could come from society with such a status. People would wonder what she'd done to end up without the support of a man: whether it was a wild and foolish feminist strike for independence or whether she had loose morals or just plain bad luck. Not that being married was any guarantee or insulation from judgement.

Vayle swallowed, every brave and independent reason she wanted to cling to crumbling away, knowing in her heart she could at the very least consider the outcome for Angelos, ensuring her child wouldn't carry even a hint of the stigma that shouldn't exist but still did. That he would at least have his father in his life on whatever basis they could agree on.

Wasn't that the fundamental reason she'd persisted in trying to let Nelios know he'd fathered a child—to give her child options?

And all this option would take would be to submit to a loveless, emotionless union—that or be locked in a legal battle which outcome she could foretell, having just been through a battle with Nelios only a year ago.

Well, she thought a little hysterically, perhaps not entirely emotionless. Because she felt very many things in this moment, including the almost childish urge to scream that life wasn't fair. But, to be fair, she'd landed herself in this situation. She'd chosen to sleep with him. To lose herself in wild, unfettered lust.

But, perhaps childishly, she could blame him for being entirely too handsome, too charismatic and too dynamic with those chiselled good looks, capable hands and sinful lips! He was a sorcerer who'd enchanted her and he deserved some of her ire for it.

'Careful, there, you look as if you're about to claw my face off. Not quite how I imagined you responding to my proposal,' he rasped, eyes backlit with a blaze she couldn't quite interpret. Which made her *feel* some more.

She breathed in and forced her clenched hands to unfurl. 'How did you imagine it, then? Me, prostrate at your feet in abject gratitude?'

His head tilted and, damn him, his eyes glinted in mocking appreciation. 'Hmm. Now there's an idea.'

'Well, dream on. It's not going to happen.' The snap in her voice drew Angelos's attention. Happily gorged on his meal, he lifted his head, his brown eyes staring raptly before, cracking a milky smile, he turned his attention to Nelios.

Father and son commenced another staring match, which continued even as Nelios lifted his hand and slowly, for the very first time, brushed his fingers over his son's crown. The breath that shuddered out of him—the briefest insight into his raw possessiveness and determination as he cradled his son's head—cemented the reluctant belief that, no, Nelios would never harm their baby. That perhaps, far from that, he would strive to move mountains for his flesh and blood.

Should she choose to stand in his way, she might well be obliterated in the process.

So she chose. *Wisely*.

The stately manor in the Hertfordshire countryside was her choice of wedding venue, because Nelios had wanted to whisk her off to Greece.

That had been Vayle's second demand. Her first had been that Agnes attend their wedding. It had been non-negotiable.

The third demand, that had caused a near-seismic event, had by far been her boldest. Part of her agreement to become Mrs Nelios Petralis for the best part of the next two decades was that Nelios have five-hour-long meetings with his mother, all to take place within the next three months—also non-negotiable.

He'd levelled a withering look at her that she'd withstood while burping his son, then, when the heavens had rewarded her efforts with Angelos's loud burp, she'd enquired whether Nelios wanted to hold his son for the first time.

Ne, he'd said, his voice deep, shaken.

She'd handed him a wide-eyed Angelos. He'd surged to his feet and prowled the living room, all lithe power and grace, his eyes locked on his son. After the third circuit, when he'd dropped the softest, lingering kiss on Angelos's forehead and exhaled long and hard, he'd stopped in front of her, looked down with that primitive, possessive light in his eyes and said huskily, 'You have a deal.'

Lawyers had been summoned and papers drawn up. She'd received an email with a veritable laundry list of what needed to be done by her and by his army of minions before they exchanged vows in a matter of weeks.

And here she was, watching the final touches being put to the transformed grounds which would host the exclusive one-hundred-strong list of Nelios Petralis's honoured guests. Well, ninety-eight to her two: Agnes and Angelos.

She forced down a mouthful of granola and returned to the gorgeous suite decorated with a blushing bride-to-be in mind. Vayle would've snorted under her breath at how far she was from that description if the knot beneath her breastbone didn't rub her the wrong way every time she tried to take a breath. It wasn't heartache, or wishes harboured and discarded. Definitely not. She was going into this thing with her eyes wide open.

Far from not wanting his son, as she had thought, Nelios was in full claiming mode. She still didn't know if he'd known of his existence or not—a fact yet to be established.

She was doing what was best for her son. And her 'surrogate mother'. Agnes breaking down in happy tears on hearing the news had cemented the issue for Vayle. On that, Vayle's heart was at ease. What she was not at ease with was the way her heart behaved around Nelios. And not just her heart. A frisson seized her whole being whenever he was within touching distance, like the echo of a tuning fork.

It was why she'd requested a special clause in their agreement: *no sex*. A demand Nelios had treated with a sliver of sardonicism and a flash of taut rancour before his impressive self-control had reasserted itself, followed by an imperious wave of dismissal, and he'd signed his name with a flourish, sealing their fate.

After checking in on Angelos, judging she had about half an hour before he woke, she stepped into the lavish bathroom and indulged in a luxurious shower, hoping it would dilute some of the jitters swarming her belly.

Predictably, as her hands moved over her body, she was struck by an ominous voice demanding to know if she'd been wise to add that clause to their agreement. Because she had *liked* having sex with Nelios, and eighteen years was a very long time to condemn herself to celibacy.

But, as she braced her hand against the wall and tried to resist taking care of the urgent need pounding between her legs, she accepted that part of why she'd felt so devastated by what had happened the next morning, besides the humiliation, was because their night together had meant something to her besides a physical exchange of desire and pleasure.

There was wisdom to knowing which battles were unwinnable. And, as much as it thrilled her very blood to go toe to toe with Nelios over his domineering manner, she recognised that the subject of sex was one she would do well to stay away from.

Because sex with him had transcended her every reality.

It had sent her to a place where she was at her weakest, where she would've happily handed over more than just her body to him for the chance to experience it again. And, yes, that too was the reason his rejection had hit her all the more viciously. So, sex would have to remain off the table so she could guard more important things, such as her sanity. *Her heart.*

Her son didn't disappoint her and rose like clockwork from his mid-morning nap the moment she stepped out of the shower, demanding a feed. She used it gratefully to occupy her mind as the time ticked down to when the couturier and her small army would descend on her a mere hour later.

By midday, Vayle was fully installed in the ivory Italian duchesse-satin gown with a pleated corset top and sleeves that sat just off her shoulders. The necklace of round-cut diamonds set in white gold, with a pink teardrop diamond pendant that rested on the pulse point at her throat, had been delivered last night courtesy of Nelios. Matching earrings graced her lobes and a simple bracelet, her right wrist.

The team of attendants had just finished arranging her hair in an elaborate, tasteful chignon when she looked up and saw Agnes standing several feet away, a tearful smile on her face.

She twisted in her seat, her own smile growing tentatively.

'Can we have some privacy, please? Just for a few moments.'

She rose as the attendants relocated to the living room, and approached the older woman, her hands outstretched.

Agnes's lips wobbled a little bit more before she firmed them. 'You look beautiful, *agapita*.'

'So do you,' Vayle murmured.

They exchanged a fond look before the usual wave of anguish washed over Agnes's face. 'I may have lost a son I will never get back, but I gained a daughter despite all my failings. I love you, Vayle. You and Angelos, you mean everything to me. I'm saying it now in case I never get the chance to atone for my…'

'Of course you will have many more chances. I'm not going anywhere and neither is your grandson. Concentrate on working things out with your son.'

Desolation crossed her face. 'What if he never forgives me?'

'You won't know until you try.'

She sucked in a shuddery breath. 'What did I ever do to deserve you?' Her eyes brimmed with tears.

Vayle blinked away threatening tears of her own. 'You saved me. You loved me even though I wasn't yours. Family is originally blood, but often it's also the people we meet and help and love along the way. You didn't turn your back on me when you could have. You made me feel more loved than my own flesh and blood did. I will always love you for that. But you also need to not give up on the other family you do have.'

Wrenching anguish kept hold of Agnes for the longest time. Watching her battle through it brought a heavier lump to Vayle's throat. But the woman who had given Nelios Petralis life, who had had some hand in shaping him despite his insistence that only his trauma had forged him, finally emerged. A steel spine shimmered into being, a little fragile and bendable perhaps, but steel nonetheless. With a firm nod, Agnes grabbed one last tissue and dabbed her damp eyes. 'We've kept him waiting long enough. Let's get our game faces back on and you up the aisle, yes?'

Vayle gulped as the butterflies reawakened. 'Yes.'

Agnes walked her down the aisle—another condition Vayle had insisted upon, especially since Andreas the Ogre was Nelios's best man. In the rush to this wedding, she'd crossed paths with Andreas only twice. She'd sensed he had something to say to her but she'd distanced herself from the interaction, not wanting her already unsettled emotions to be toppled by his caustic opinions. On both occasions she'd been with Nelios, who had also seemed reluctant to leave her alone with his right-hand man.

So, yes, she chalked it up to a win as she proceeded arm-in-arm with Agnes down the aisle.

Of course, all thoughts of winning, losing or otherwise fled the second she clapped eyes on Nelios, in the finest hand-made suit, with his hair combed off his forehead to better display the sheer force of his male beauty. Everything faded to sepia while he blazed in vivid, living colour.

She couldn't even pick one thing that reigned supreme above another: his eyes, his jaw, his unabashed ferocity; the pristine whiteness of his collar against the rich dark-blue of his wedding suit; or the resolute power that snaked out and compelled her to him, her every step seeming to echo his silent, unyielding intonation of *mine, mine, mine...*

She scarcely felt the exquisite bouquet being tugged from her hold, or barely saw Agnes and Andreas retreat to their seats.

She did feel the electric power of his touch when he took her hand and propelled her that last step to his side. Felt every word of the simple yet weighty vows they exchanged. He slid the diamond-and-platinum wedding band onto her finger that perfectly matched the priceless engagement ring, drew her into his arms, fused his lips to hers and rasped, 'It is done.'

Oh yes; Vayle very much felt that too.

He was married.

As he led his new bride across the dance floor, Nelios finally allowed the landscape to settle; allowed himself to open his mind to what he'd negotiated for these past weeks. What he'd vowed when he'd held his son for the first time.

As he'd looked into Angelos's eyes, and sworn to do the polar opposite of what had been done to him, he knew he'd allow very little to stand in his way. Even if it meant having to deal with his mother and hear more lies from her treacherous lips.

To gain his son, he realised he would even withstand that torture, and more. It would only be a few hours of his life, after all, compared to a lifetime of ensuring that his offspring never suffered as he had. As exchanges went, Nelios believed he'd got the better part of the bargain. So why did that chafing still lurk within him? Why did it feel as if this mission wasn't quite complete?

As he guided Vayle back across the dance floor, his gaze connected with his friend's. Andreas still hadn't lost that shadowed tension in his eyes ever since their heated conversation a month ago after he'd delivered Vayle and Angelos back to her apartment.

It took a lot for his only friend to accept blame, because he'd rarely ever stepped out of line. So Nelios had been mildly stunned when Andreas had come to him and immediately offered his sincere apologies for keeping Nelios from Angelos. He'd thought he was doing the right thing by having his friend's back, thinking he was protecting Nelios from a threat they'd both faced before from women who'd made spurious claims of being pregnant by them, with only grasping avarice in mind. In their world, gold-diggers like that were ten a penny. Andreas had thought he was dealing with yet another one in Buenos Aires, so he'd ignored Vayle's calls, had had her emails deleted unread and had discarded her letter.

Nelios truly believed it had been a misunderstanding on his friend's part, and he'd had to accept that he too had dropped the ball, when all was said and done. He'd also had to accept that missing his son's momentous milestones thus far was perhaps his penance. He'd grudgingly let it go.

But clearly Andreas hadn't, if the guilty grimace he slanted Nelio's way was any indication.

'Things not all rosy in friendship land?'

He dropped his gaze to Vayle and, despite the tension lurking in her own features, some of the chafing eased. His own grimace he kept to himself. He hadn't fooled himself into believing this wedding would be an especially happy occasion but, while he didn't really care what his specially selected business and social acquaintances thought, he didn't want to start off his marriage anything but impeccably.

Her eyes held a faint wariness but it was the fire in them that snagged at him. That promised that, whatever lay ahead of them, it would be far from boring.

Nelios found himself anticipating that challenge, even welcoming it. His eyes dropped lower to the diamonds encircling her neck and the hint of cleavage that made other parts of him tighten. 'Have I said how exquisite you look?'

The concoction of ivory satin elevated her glow, and the faint flush to her cheeks and the diamonds only harnessed her stunning beauty. But more than that there was an ephemeral quality to this woman that had enthralled him from the start. That, he was a little disturbed to admit, he'd gone searching for in others, and had failed to find.

'Not going to answer my question?' she replied.

'The issue has been explained and resolved,' he offered.

'Has it? And no one bothered to tell me?' she said sarcastically. 'What is your deal with Andreas anyway?'

His gaze sharpened. 'What?'

She shrugged and his gaze moved over her smooth skin again, hunger slowly prowling its restlessness through him.

'I looked him up like any sane person would when you started your antics. I looked you both up, in fact. There is very little about him on the Internet.'

'Because he is a private man. But our origins crossed

at a crucial point which aided the forging of an unbreakable friendship.'

Curiosity sparkled in her eyes and Nelios couldn't drag his gaze away. 'What happened?' She used that same soft, empathetic voice she always used when advocating for Agnes. He shouldn't have fallen for it, yet he felt a certain...*give* in his chest.

Which he immediately suppressed by shaking his head. 'This is neither the time nor the place for confessions, *yineka mou*.'

'What does "*yineka mou*" mean?' she muttered.

He felt that hungry flame burning brighter as he stared down into her eyes. 'It means "my wife". And I would rather talk about us, not Andreas.'

Was it his imagination or did a shiver run through her? Dropping his gaze, he saw the pulse at her throat speed up and his whole body felt charged, that anticipation building. Which was why he almost growled when a hand tapped his shoulder.

Speak of the devil.

'It's my turn to dance with the bride, I believe,' Andreas murmured.

The right, civil thing to do would be to hand over his wife. But Nelios didn't feel particularly civil.

'No can do. I'm not quite done dancing with my wife. If you're in need of a dance partner, Agnes is free, I believe.'

His friend barely managed to keep his surprise from showing, and after a moment nodded and turned to Vayle.

'In case later isn't good for your husband either,' he said with a hint of a wryness, 'I'd like to take this opportunity to apologise for my actions over the last year. I've been rather...over-zealous in my gatekeeping.'

Vayle watched him and let him stew for a few several

seconds before she nodded. 'Apology accepted. As long as you're cordial to Agnes, we won't have a problem.'

The baffled knot in Nelios's gut tightened as his friend walked away to do his wife's bidding.

'You're staring again.'

He bit his tongue against a trite response about her beauty, or something primeval, such as he was allowed to look at her now she was his. Instead he found himself blurting, 'You really do insist on seeing the good in everyone, don't you?'

She stiffened for a moment, then lanced him a challenging glance. 'I'm hardly Mary Poppins, but really, isn't stomping about gathering all the dark clouds around you exhausting for you and everyone else?'

For the wildest, most absurd second, Nelios felt laughter bubbling up in his chest at the image she conjured up. And perhaps she caught a glimpse of it, because her tension eased and her eyes dwelled on his face for much longer than he was strictly comfortable with. But the moment she glanced over his shoulder, her eyes softening at seeing Agnes on Andreas's arm, Nelios wanted her attention back on him.

'I assure you, it's not a chore or burdensome at all,' he drawled, then exhaled steadily when her eyes returned to his. 'Thunderstorms keep everyone on their toes. But they also bring cleansing rain and new starts. In the past, I've had no choice but to forge several of my own.'

Her eyes softened further and Nelios felt the ground beneath him soften along with it, like clouds lifting him, making him feel…buoyant for the first time in a very long time. It was a deceptively addictive feeling. One he knew he needed to resist.

But maybe not just yet.

One song drifted into another as his new wife looked up at him. 'As great as that may be, surely sunshine after all that rain makes things look and feel so much better?'

Again a touch of humour lightened his chest. 'What next, Vayle—a debate about the benefit of rainbows?'

She blinked at him in mock annoyance. 'I love rainbows, and I won't have them disparaged. So why don't I go about sunshining to my heart's content and you thundercloud all you want? And if we happen to clash...' She shrugged smooth shoulders, her body moving under his touch, reminding him what lay beneath the layers of satin.

Just a little while ago he'd speculated that this marriage would be far from boring, but maybe he'd underestimated that sentiment. Maybe there was room for...more. Such as renegotiating the no-sex clause he'd foolishly agreed to...

'Thank you for allowing her to be here.'

Humour and thoughts of sex and rainbows fled as he followed her gaze to Agnes. 'She has my wife to thank for that.' Why did using that term settle something primal inside him?

'I know. But you still could've objected. I know what you're capable of.'

His eyes sharpened on her face. 'Is that supposed to be an accusation?' he asked with a touch of disappointment he sensed was directly connected to losing the pleasant connection they'd shared a minute ago. The dismaying hollow in his belly wanted that warmth back. He was disgruntled to admit that the *exhausting* weight of this bitterness he harboured for Agnes—the constant anger-tinged shadows of grief for not being granted the opportunity to face his father and show him the man he'd become *despite* him—was all so very *exhausting*. *Thee mou*, there was that word again. His wife had planted it in his head, and now it was all he could feel.

She firmed her lips. 'It was truth-stating.'

He barely stopped his teeth from gritting. 'It's our wedding day, Vayle. Let's not ruin it by arguing.'

She nodded. 'Agreed. But you will still talk to your mother, yes? Attempt to put the past behind you?'

The earlier rush of winning, of embracing his new landscape, dimmed a little as he looked into her eyes. What if he failed? What if this would be him two decades from now, gazing at his own son after having failed him?

No. That would never happen. Not as long as he had breath in his body and a memory to keep him firmly on the new path he intended to choose. Snatching his flailing emotions back under control, he refocused on Vayle.

'That's what you negotiated on her behalf. So, yes, I'll stick to it even if I don't hold much hope of being swayed by anything she has to say.' His smile felt mirthless and tight. 'But you'll do well not to push me.'

The end of the music punctuated his statement and he escorted her back to their table, despising that fervent wish to wind the clock back to five minutes ago.

CHAPTER SEVEN

IT WAS THE height of pathetic behaviour to wander about like a hapless, jilted lover on his own wedding night. It was even more tragic to lie in bed on a night he should've treated like every other night, considering he'd only married for the sake of his son, and wish for his new wife's warm, delectable body next to his.

He'd left her in that bed in Buenos Aires because he'd tried to convince himself he was done with her. And he'd almost been convinced of that.

Until all the talk of thunderclouds, sunshine and rainbows. To his disarming surprise, he'd found himself dwelling on that conversation for the rest of the wedding reception, wondering if there wasn't some merit to Vayle's argument. Wondering if this woman—who, against all odds, had chosen to keep his child and had striven to let him know he was to become a father because it was *the right thing to do*—wasn't the enemy after all.

Impatient with himself—and, yes, finding it hard to accept he might have read her wrong—Nelios rose and tugged on his dressing gown. He told himself he didn't hope she was losing sleep too; that maybe, if she happened to be awake, there would be a repeat of when she'd charged after him that night in Buenos Aires, slammed those small but firm hands on his chest and demanded he hear her out.

And, no, he didn't hold his breath at all when he pulled open his door... To an empty corridor.

Ne, he was truly pathetic.

Shoving his hands into his pockets, he picked a destination and stalked downstairs towards the ballroom of the manor, his footsteps echoing off the polished parquet floor like mocking taunts. Just hours ago, the room had been brimming with champagne, laughter and the glittering presence of his guests. Now it echoed with silence and the weight of his own frustration.

It was his wedding night, damn it. He should be upstairs with Vayle, tracing the delicate lace of her dress as he peeled it away, kissing down the curve of her neck and watching the firelight flicker over skin he longed to reacquaint himself with. Instead, he'd been banished by his own stupid agreement to what now felt like the dumbest clause ever written into a pre-nup.

No sex...for *years*.

At the time, it had felt like a minor detail—an odd little addendum she'd requested with that careful tone of someone testing boundaries. He'd said yes with barely a pause, more focused on sealing the deal than questioning her motives. He hadn't expected it to feel so vexing. So *immediate*.

Now, hindsight clawed at him like regret soaked in acid. What had he been thinking—that restraint would impress her? Win her over faster so she'd sign the document? He wanted his wife. Perhaps not desperately—he wasn't an untried schoolboy, after all—but the need was there, residing beneath his not-so-calm surface. It was aching, maddening. And she wasn't miles away. She was right there.

He glanced towards the sweeping staircase, half-tempted

to storm up there and tear up the clause himself. But what would that prove—that he couldn't honour a promise? That he was just another man ruled by his loins? No.

He clenched his jaw and turned back towards the bar, grabbing a bottle and pouring himself two fingers of scotch with more force than necessary. The amber liquid sloshed in the glass, mocking him.

Years...

Nelios took a slow sip, accepting that, for once in his life, he'd perhaps accepted a challenge he might not win.

He slept like crap, as predicted, dreaming of a house and living room he hadn't seen in over two decades; of a place he'd believed was his sanctuary but had turned out to be false; of three adults deciding his fate, two of whom should never even have considered the abandonment they'd planned.

They'd sacrificed him for *material things*.

Nelios was aware there was a trough of questions still to be answered, but it wasn't as if he hadn't lain awake endless nights, parsing every reason and accepting there was no rationale that could explain such a decision. *Besides greed...*

But he'd promised to hear Agnes out, he recalled as he abandoned his bed at dawn in favour of the study that came with the manor, feeling a lot more like himself as he faced a few hours of satisfying work. When the sound of husky laughter reached him an hour after sunrise, he rose from his desk and padded to the corner of the Edwardian bay windows that overlooked the terrace. Where Vayle was about to have her breakfast with a content-looking Angelos reclining in his rocking cot.

Tossing his tablet onto the desk, he walked out of the study. Her head snapped his way and he braced himself for the unique fizz of tangling with Vayle... Petralis. When no skirmish came his way, he told himself he wasn't disappointed. That cordial relations worked for him. Going over to Angelos, he squatted next to the rocking cot, his insides turning over when soft brown eyes met his. '*Kaliméra*, Angelos.'

His son blinked, then burbled at him.

He turned to his wife. '*Kaliméra*.'

'Good morning,' she murmured.

'Did you sleep well?'

A curious look whispered over her face before she shrugged. 'Not really. Strange beds and all that.'

He was a bastard to hope she'd experienced a sliver of his frustration as he gestured at the breakfast table. 'May I join you?'

She shrugged again. 'It's your manor for the duration. I can hardly stop you, so go ahead.'

Curbing a curious smile at the cute impertinence, he pulled out a chair and sat down. A waiter approached and Nelios discovered he was ravenous. He made his request then sat back, seeing absolutely nothing wrong with letting his eyes wander over his new wife. So what if the label sent a pulse of pure primitive delight through him? In the light of day, his regret about that no-sex clause had receded. He had his son exactly where he wanted him, with a cast-iron assurance that the trauma and torments of the parents would never be visited upon the son. A reality for which he would raze whole worlds to the ground.

So a small but lavish wedding, a ring on his finger and a woman who now bore his name was a fair price to pay.

Are you sure? You're so cocky now, in the light of day. But night will come again, all too soon.

He swatted the question away and fixed his eyes on her,

cataloguing her from head to toe so he wouldn't have to dwell on the mocking voice.

The weak summer sun graced her with shafts of light, but as to whether her skin glowed because of it, or it was a leftover from her pregnancy, he didn't wonder about for long. Because, with each second his gaze lingered on her, the higher he felt the need to sit forward and trail his fingers over her cheek, jaw and over the pulse beating steadily at her throat.

He'd tasted her right there. Had made her breath hitch and her lips part with hunger that he'd greedily and decadently taken delight in assuaging.

'You?'

He shifted his gaze to her face. 'Hmm?'

'I asked how you slept.'

He saw no reason to prevaricate, so he didn't. 'Shoddily. For various reasons.'

He waited, for what he wasn't sure. And, when faint colour stained her cheeks and she looked away, he got that urge to smile. He, who never smiled unless it was at an opponent's expense.

'Such as?'

His humour disappeared. Since she was the main reason his sleep had been disturbed, he picked the most pressing reason and offered it to her. 'The fact that it was our wedding night doesn't count?'

Her eyes widened a touch and searched his. 'We agreed on celibacy.'

'*Ne*, but perhaps the question is, why the need to stipulate it in the first place?'

'I'm not rehashing a done deal with you, Nelios,' she said a little hurriedly.

His pulse jumped at his name falling from her lips. 'No? I thought that was right in your wheelhouse.'

'And didn't you insist I should be happy with what I got?'

Hoist by his own petard.

'Have you spoken to Agnes yet?' she blurted.

The douse of ice on his emotions irritated him. 'If you must know, we encountered one another this morning,' he said, recalling the very brief interaction with his mother in the hallway when he'd first come downstairs. He'd forgotten she was an early riser too. Or that perhaps, like him, she'd had a sleepless night, only for different reasons.

'And?'

Nelios wasn't certain which disturbed him more—that he'd agreed to this to please Vayle, or that he hadn't walked away from his mother with as much emotional detachment as he would've wished. Especially when she'd insisted there were supposedly important details she needed to give him. 'I agreed to talk. I didn't agree to giving you a play-by-play.'

Her face fell just before she sent him a disappointed glare. And he absolutely *did not* squirm in his seat… It was the brisk July air, which should've been wonderfully temperate, as it was in Greece, but instead bordered on cold. It reminded him why he disliked the intemperate English weather, and he seized on the other subject on his mind.

'There's no rush, of course, but it would be good for you to get a feel of the Nelios Group before you make a decision about which hotel you wish to work in. I thought we'd start in Greece; introduce Angelos to his other homeland. Then wherever in the world you wish to go next.'

Her glare lessened. 'Really?'

Was it the sun or were her eyes always this luminous, this incredibly breathtaking? *'Ne,'* he confirmed a little gruffly.

She grew contemplative far too quickly. 'I don't want to leave Agnes for endless days.'

He ignored the chafing in his chest. 'Then we'll remain in Europe for the time being,' he assured her. 'Start the tour in southern Italy, then go to Apeiron.'

'I've never heard of that.'

'Very few people have because it's my private island in Greece. We can start from there instead of Italy, if you wish.'

It wasn't his imagination that caught a glitter of pleasure in her eyes because something flipped in his belly. And when the look evaporated he was struck with a fervent need to regain it.

'What does "Apeiron" mean?'

'Several things in Greek, but for my purposes it means "infinite".'

The glitter slowly returned, weaker than before but there. 'Because you believe your mightiness is infinite?'

Was she teasing him? The belly-flip recurred. 'Exactly so.'

He caught the twitch at the corner of her plump lips just before she turned away to shower attention on their son. He told himself he wasn't jealous; that he was perfectly content just to watch their interaction; enjoyed how naturally she doted on him and saw to his every need. How…good she was with him.

But all the while Nelios was stingingly aware of the hunger prowling within him, seeking satiation. Of the voice repeating yet again, asking himself why the hell he'd agreed to that stupid, *stupid* celibacy clause.

Vayle hated herself for missing Nelios even before he had walked away after devouring his breakfast, with a request she be ready to leave by lunchtime. More so for the giddiness that took hold of her entire being, making her feel as if she was permanently plugged into a low-voltage current. Even when Agnes joined them to play with Angelos before the arranged driver took her back home, Vayle could barely concentrate on their conversation.

'You'll love Greece.' The usual sadness tinged her words as Vayle kissed her goodbye.

Vayle finally forced herself to focus. 'Will you be okay?'

Agnes nodded, her gaze drifting over Vayle's shoulder, no doubt looking for the son who was resolutely ignoring her. 'Things aren't going as quickly as I'd like but... I have hope.'

A lump rose in her throat and she embraced Agnes. 'I'll call as soon as I can.'

Agnes shook her head. 'Don't hurry. This is a new beginning for you. And I have a feeling my son needs you more than he's willing to let on. Take your time; treasure this new life you're beginning.'

Vayle shook her head, clenching her belly against the acute yearning that struck her. 'It's not like that, Agnes. You know why we married. It's just for Angelos's sake.' She peered deeper into Agnes's eyes, hoping to see understanding, perhaps even an agreement that it was truly unwise to build hopes on a marriage of convenience.

But Agnes gave a small but confident smile. 'Don't assume a door is locked before you've turned the handle, *agapolou*.'

The words echoed in her head long after they'd boarded a helicopter to the very airport where she'd breached security to stow away on Nelios's jet.

And if the crew, which included Capaldi but was minus

Andreas, was stunned to see her board with a baby in tow, they kept it well hidden. In fact, they seemed to forget her existence just as quickly, their attention fully absorbed by Angelos, now learning to smile and collecting hearts in his little fists as he offered one toothless smile after another.

Vayle blinked as Nelios produced a snazzy pair of baby headphones and slotted them over Angelos's head. 'Noise-cancelling to protect his ears,' he muttered, then dropped a kiss on his son's head once the device was in place. 'There's a cot in the back too, for when he needs it.'

That softening threatened again. For some reason, Nelios's demand two weeks ago as to whether he was a monster, and how her instincts had immediately rejected that idea, flared across her senses. She realised she was staring at him, unable to look away as the plane gained speed.

And, no, she didn't trick herself with the lie that it was the steep take-off that took her breath away. It was Nelios Petralis—fearsome, ruthless, towering and larger than life, but with a not so insubstantial vein of humanity buried beneath it all. That was the man who held her in a thrall she feared would overwhelm her if she didn't find a way to break it.

So she was grateful that they had indeed decided to start the tour in southern Italy rather than the luxurious splendour of his Greek island.

Nelios XIV glittered on the shores of the Ionian Sea, a masterpiece of graceful marble arches, sprawling hallways, hidden alcoves and centuries-old charm. The staff displayed the right amount of haughtiness, pride and reverence to their guests.

'Something amusing you?' Nelios drawled beside her as

they followed the impeccably dressed manager who personally escorted them to their suite.

'I think you might be coming a lowly second to the adoration of your own creation. They love your hotel more than they love you.'

He shrugged, supremely confident in his appeal even as a spasm of some strange emotion washed over his face. 'It's a lucky thing then that I don't particularly desire to be loved.'

'That's rubbish. Everyone desires to be loved, on some level.' Her vehemence on the subject shocked her a little. As did the rolling quakes that started in her chest and unfurled until they engulfed her whole body. Because it was almost as if his observation…frightened her. As if he had shut a door she very much wanted to remain open.

His sharp look confirmed that, yes, she'd been too fervent. That perhaps he'd even found it objectionable. 'Desires are one thing. Accepting the reality of the hand we're dealt is quite another.'

'You haven't struck me as the type to sit back and let someone else deal your cards, so that argument is hogwash.' Why was she pushing this? Why not just accept his words at face value and save herself the trouble?

Don't assume a door is locked before you've turned the handle…

His footsteps had slowed to match hers, their escort several steps ahead. 'So you believe I should scramble about, petitioning for affection and attention?'

Her gaze dropped to the wide platinum band encircling his ring finger. The band she'd placed there. He followed her gaze, his features tightening again. 'Or I supposed that boat has sailed for me, *ne*?'

She wanted to make a flippant remark about his potential to be supremely eligible again eighteen years from now, when by their agreement she would be free to walk away. When she doubted he would still be anything but jaw-dropping, even as a silver fox. But the words stuck in her throat, the vice around her chest constricting until she was terrified to take a full breath.

Luckily, they'd arrived at their designated suite. And, when the double doors were thrown open and she stepped inside, a different urgency took hold. She barely managed to bite her tongue until the manager had finished his elaborate spiel about the endless amenities available to them—including a makeshift nursery specially set up for Angelos—and left.

'Is there a problem?' Nelios drawled.

'Do I need to point it out? There's only one bed.'

His jaw clenched. 'It's the height of the summer season. I can have the second penthouse guests thrown out, if you wish?'

'No, I don't wish, and don't make me sound like a demanding harridan. We spent our wedding night in separate beds. What makes you think I want that situation to change today?'

His nostrils flared. 'I'm well aware how we spent our wedding night, *yineka mou*.'

Tension swirled as they froze, examining one another as if they were preying cobras waiting for the first sign of weakness to strike.

'Nelios…'

'The neutral venue for our wedding was quite different from my company, where there are eyes and ears everywhere. I didn't think it prudent to crank the rumour mill this soon, especially around employees you might be managing in the near future. Do you?'

Put like that, it made sound sense. If she could only manage to put her sensibilities aside long enough to remember they'd signed an agreement to which they should be able to adhere with minimum fuss regardless of where they slept, since they were adults.

But... As she looked around, she couldn't ignore the distinct sense that the suite had been specially prepared with newlyweds in mind. Such as the console table brimming with an extra-large bouquet of her favourite blush-rose flowers. Or the champagne chilling in an ice-bucket next to the picturesque fireplace. Or the matching 'his and hers' silk dressing gowns and slippers draped enticingly near the bathroom doors.

The room screamed romance.

Her senses screamed for deliverance before she did something foolish. Angelos wriggling his irritation gave her the perfect out. He'd been an angel all through the two-hour flight and transfer from airport to hotel. And she was ready to shower him with praise for it. 'I need to feed Angelos and get him down for his nap.'

Nelios stared at her for a taut moment then, the corner of his mouth twitching, he ran a hand over his son's head, a gesture he seemed to crave more and more, following it with a kiss. 'Fine. We will do the tour later.'

Watching him turn away, she was struck again by that tightening in her chest. She hated watching Nelios walk away from her. Which was absurd...wasn't it?

When he returned an hour later, it was with Capaldi in tow. Like Andreas at their wedding, he was now less rigid, even bordering on smiling.

'If you're comfortable leaving Angelos to sleep, Capaldi will stay with him,' Nelios said.

At her obvious surprise, Capaldi shrugged. 'I have three young ones of my own. A sleeping baby is a breeze.'

He might have been a near-stranger to her but he wasn't to Nelios. And, after seeing the closeness between Nelios, Andreas and Capaldi, Vayle found herself nodding her agreement. 'Thank you.'

Capaldi's near-smile grew more prominent. Why that made Nelios frown, she didn't get a chance to dwell on as his hand arrived at the small of her back and guided her towards the door. He conducted the tour himself, and it didn't take long to figure out that this particular hotel was run more like a sprawling, eye-wateringly exclusive private villa than the mainstream establishments under the Nelios Group umbrella. And that it was a well-oiled machine.

'I organised a late lunch for us.' He indicated the table for two laid with pristine silverware situated away from the others, with magnificent views of the pool and the glittering sea beyond.

It was gorgeous beyond words but that wasn't what made her heart race. It was the intimacy of it. It was how her entire being came *alive* with yearning at the thought of spending more time with Nelios—the very man she'd never expected to set eyes on again only a month ago. And the alarming thought that part of the reason she'd already decided against working in this hotel was because it wasn't where Nelios would be.

Because she wanted to be around him for Angelos's sake, she added hastily; nothing else.

'Vayle?' he pressed.

She moved towards the table, then paused. 'Is Capaldi...?'

'He'll let us know if we're needed.' His gaze dropped to her chest. 'Unless you wish to return for a different reason?'

His voice pulsed with…something. Her cheeks flamed. She hadn't missed the breast pump near the changing table when she'd put Angelos to bed.

'No, I don't.' She cleared her throat and moved to the chair he pulled out for her. 'We haven't even discussed where we will live. Or does that not matter to you?' she asked once they'd sat down. It wasn't an accusation, just a means of gaining insight into this man whose child she'd birthed and whose name she now carried but whom she barely knew, except in the biblical sense. God, why had she thought about that right now?

His eyes lingered for too long on her heated cheeks before meeting hers. 'I'm able to work anywhere in the world, but I primarily base myself in Athens. And, no, England won't be my first choice,' he added with the hint of an edge that said it wasn't just the weather he objected to.

Vayle wanted to pry more into his meeting with Agnes but she held her tongue as the waiter approached and they ordered their food. 'So do you have men like Capaldi and Andreas littered all over the world to aid you in your empire-building?' she started as a means to fill in the watchful silence, but as she said the words she realised she genuinely wanted to know.

He handed the wine list back to the sommelier and fixed his eyes on her after she declined wine in favour of flavoured water. 'Not so many as you might think, but enough that I trust implicitly, yes.'

'And how did they earn your trust?'

His lips tightened and his gaze slanted over her shoulder to rest on the horizon. The tension building told her to leave the subject alone but that urgent throb in her chest said she couldn't. Or perhaps it was the echo of Agnes's words pushing her when she would've withdrawn at any other time.

She sucked in a steadying breath and plunged ahead. 'I know you've given me the broad strokes of what happened the day the foster carer came to your house,' she murmured.

His mouth twisted. 'A truth you thought was a lie, or at best a grand exaggeration, even after feeling a measure of rejection from your own father?' he asked a little bitterly.

Her heart squeezed, for him and for her. 'Will you tell me what happened?' she pushed softly.

His unyielding expression didn't lessen. 'What purpose would it serve?'

She toyed with the crystal glass dampening with condensation from the cold water. 'Beyond wanting a better understanding of the person I'll be parenting my son with? How about so I'm not caught flat-footed and pitied next time I have a conversation with one of your trusted friends? Or are you happy to let everyone wonder why we don't know the bare facts, never mind the most important things, about each other?'

Dark-coffee eyes examined her for a full minute, his upper body relaxed against his chair in a posture of ease she knew was false. 'And all this baring of oneself and risking losing one's appetite for what should be an exceptional meal—is it to be a one-sided thing?' he drawled idly. But the taut skin around his mouth told a different story.

Her insides fluttered with nerves she hadn't felt for a very long time. And, while she knew reliving everything would reawaken a slumbering anguish, bare her failures and vulnerability to his incisive probing, part of her was eager to rise above the wounds of her past rejection, to share this part of herself with him. After all, it wasn't her heart or the strain of fevered yearning she couldn't quite stem. So it was fine...right?

'I hate the dark because part of my father's illness included adverse reaction to bright lights during his manic episodes. Lights out in my house meant things...weren't going well. Even candles bothered him.'

Nelios went statue-still, exhaling harshly as thunder rolled across his face. 'So you were forced to live in the dark when he was unwell? How long were his episodes?'

Yeah, maybe he was right about the indigestion, but even as her stomach roiled she carried on. 'Sometimes hours. Sometimes days.'

His nostrils thinned as his fury grew. 'And you were forced to endure this all on your own?' he seethed.

'After my mother died, yes. Unfortunately, he only got worse with time...until...you know what happened.'

His eyes narrowed but a layer of tension eased out of him. 'So it took the bank to make him seek help?' he asked.

She laughed caustically. 'The hotel was the only thing he cared about after my mother died, so yes, the threat of having it taken away finally got through to him.'

'And then Agnes and Tolis entered the picture,' he concluded.

'Yes.'

'And you think, because they purportedly saved you, you should go around saving everyone else?' he asked, eyebrow raised, and then a hint of regret flashed across his face when she flinched. But he didn't take it back, nor did she want him to, because there was truth rooted in his statement.

She'd nearly fallen off the edge of a cliff of despair from her inability to help her father. To be worthy enough for him to want to seek help. To be worthy of him, full-stop.

She'd failed. But a Greek couple had shown her she wasn't entirely worthless. She'd been saved by the very people her husband despised. It didn't negate her love and gratitude for them, even if she realised they too might have been flawed.

'Maybe. But it may also be because, while we both know that no one can hurt you like family can, family can also heal you, even if that family isn't necessarily your blood.'

His mouth flattened but he didn't say a word. And then their food was brought out, shattering the brittle atmosphere. He examined his plate with clear dispassion that she now felt too.

And, when he sent her speaking look, she grimaced. 'I'm not going to apologise for the timing. You asked. I answered.'

To her surprise he nodded and, rising, he stepped behind her chair. 'I'll have it sent up to our room. Maybe by the time we return, our appetites will have forgiven us.'

She bit her tongue against asking him to reciprocate, since she'd bared her painful past, the helplessness and distress she'd felt.

'I used to think there was something wrong with me. Something that made him reject his own child. Then I wondered if it was a combination of unfortunate circumstances and a mishap in genetics on my father's part that caused all that to happen.'

'No.' His voice was firm from the fury boiling off him. 'Don't excuse his actions as a genetic flaw. You say he loved your mother and yet he picked on everyone else, you included. No one bothered to stand up to him or take steps quickly enough to protect you from him. He wised up when what really mattered to him was threatened—not his child, not your mother. A pile of bricks was what he cared about most. I'd say spare yourself the efforts of forgiving him, but I sense that you already have.'

There was a searching light in his eyes as he stopped in

the hallway and peered down at her, one she couldn't escape. She didn't even need to nod or respond audibly. He knew she'd, if not healed completely, at least come to terms with her father's rejection with help from Nelios's parents.

But the censure she had expected didn't arrive. Instead he continued to search her features, as if looking for answers *he* sought.

And then he placed his hand on the small of her back, triggering a deep pulse of yearning as they neared their suite.

CHAPTER EIGHT

CAPALDI ROSE WHEN they entered, clicking off the phone he had been scrolling through.

'Nothing to report,' he said.

'Efkharisto,' Nelios murmured.

The other man nodded and left after Vayle added her thanks. Nelios followed her to check in on their son. Content to see him resting peacefully, she returned to the living room, just as a knock came on the door. He answered and the same waiter who'd served them wheeled in their lunch.

By mutual agreement they ate in near silence. Then over coffee, he levelled a steady gaze at her. 'I'm sensing this hotel isn't the one?'

She shook her head. 'No.' She gave him her earlier assessment, then carried on with her thought. 'Besides, I don't intend to leave Angelos and go back to work for the better part of a year, so I have time.'

The gleam of approval shouldn't have warmed her the way it did. She didn't need it. And yet, when he lifted his cup to drain it, she followed the movement, then waited for him to speak.

'Then should we reschedule the tour and go to Apeiron tomorrow?'

As far as she could decipher, there was something in his

voice close to a...yearning that made her heart leap. That made her readily agree, because she sensed it would give her more insight into this enigmatic man. 'Sure.'

With their meal finished, she rose, but when she walked past him he caught her wrist in a loose grip.

A little startled, both by the gesture and the way her blood rushed that little bit faster through her veins, she stumbled to a halt. 'Is there something...?'

'There was nothing wrong with you. He had a duty of care to you as his child and he failed. The flaws were all his. You know that, *ne*?' he said, a kind of deep insistence in his voice, as if he needed her to believe that.

Or maybe it was in her imagination. Because why would Nelios care what scars she'd been left with? Unless he just... cared about her?

Lightly buoyed by that thought, she bit her inner lip and blurted, 'If I do consider that, would you at least consider that your mother may have had her own flawed reasons, beyond what you believe, and hear her—?'

'Vayle...' His warning was taut. But he didn't release her or freeze her out the way he'd done in the past.

'Just keep an open mind, please?'

A lance of jagged emotion crossed his face, and something else that ludicrously resembled...*jealousy*? 'Why is this so important to you? Actually, don't answer that. I don't think I want to know.'

'Nelios, I...' She paused, wanting to reassure him but not quite knowing how. Or why helping him lift the burden of his past mattered so much to her.

Don't you know—really?

The tangle of shaking her head free of that thought and hoping he would release her culminated in a comical wobbling of her head. Because her yearning for the opposite, for him to pull her closer—preferably into his lap, to touch her, kiss her or do *more*—was chomping like ravenous pack of wolves through her. He accurately read her mind and used the connection to pull her closer until she could count the light flecks in his eyes, the fine hairs that would form his five o'clock shadow soon enough and breathe in his spicy scent. Her breath stalled in her lungs as she took another step closer.

'You done pushing?' he rasped.

'Maybe, maybe not,' she whispered.

She almost took it back when he released her. But when she didn't step away, on account of her feet refusing to move, he held her gaze for a long stretch, adjusted his body then placed his hands on her hips to pull her between his spread legs.

Her hands landed on his shoulders to steady herself. 'W-what are you doing?'

'Preventing you from scurrying off to hide in the darkness.'

'Why…do you care?'

'The elusive harmony we all search for?'

The charged little laugh escaped before she could stop it. 'I don't feel exactly harmonious when you touch me.' Vayle bit her lip as soon as the telling words escaped then, to counter it, rushed on with, 'And isn't sex forbidden in our agreement?'

'I'm doing nothing besides touching my wife. Touching is not forbidden. But let's revisit your other statement about how you feel when I touch you, *yineka mou*,' he drawled with the intense tone that made parts of her body grow heavy with wanting.

'You should forget that immediately,' she tried, knowing she shouldn't have made that unguarded admission.

The smile that curved his lips then—hot, genuine, *devastating*—made the heavy parts even heavier. 'No chance,' he replied.

She watched the brown of his eyes lighten, then heat up until they were a river of melted, dark caramel she wanted to dive headlong into. A rough sound rumbled from him and Vayle realised she was toying with the hair at his nape, and he…he was leaning into her touch.

That tiny evidence of her power was like a drug to her system. She stepped forward, her head falling forward and her breathing fractured to pieces as his grip tightened.

'Do it,' he invited. *Dared*.

And, with that expertly pushed button, Vayle kissed him while the sun dappled around them, the salt-and-flowers-laden air swirled sultrily, and an urgent whisper at the back of her mind demanded to know what the hell she was doing. A voice she actively ignored. Because she remembered this magic, yearned for a repeat.

And, as she'd secretly longed for him to do, when he took control and swept his tongue forcefully between her lips, seeking entry, she gave in with a lustful sigh and let him stoke the fire sweeping between her legs. At some point her fingers curled into his hair and gripped tightly, and she heard him grunt as she moaned her delight, dancing closer to the edge of that cliff spiked with dire warnings.

She was all for ignoring them when a sharp cry ripped them apart. For a stupefying moment, Vayle wondered if it was a wounded animal or a unique bird's cry. Then, eyes widening, she fully registered the sound. She started to step back. His fingers convulsed on her hips, staying her for another moment as he dragged his lips across hers one last time.

'I feel entirely ordinary now, as I believe I'm not the first man to be cock-blocked by his child.'

The wry amusement glinting in his eyes arrested her for several more seconds until Angelos cried out again, his indignation growing.

'I... We should...umm...'

'Go,' he said, adjusting himself with zero self-consciousness, while she writhed in a sea of volcanic need and surging alarm.

They'd been married for less than forty-eight hours of an agreed minimum of eighteen years. And here she was, fighting the strongest urge to have sex that she'd ever felt in her life. A little more than alarmed by her own surging emotions, she hurried away, gladly evolving into mummy mode.

She was just done feeding Angelos and about to change him when Nelios strolled into the nursery, crossing the room to her side.

'I will do it,' he said. He started to reach for the nappy. Then he paused, a twinge of embarrassment crossing his face. 'Show me how.'

Three tiny words. But oh, how powerfully they ploughed through her defences. So much so she could barely speak as she talked him through his first nappy change, with the standard warning about ensuring the correct positioning so he didn't get accidentally doused. And she spotted his supremely triumphant look from the corner of her eye when he deftly completed the task.

She remained a little shaken when she excused herself early evening, leaving Angelos with his father so she could video-call Agnes, relieved when the other woman smiled into the phone camera.

'I thought I might come to Athens soon.'

Vayle's heart leapt but, remembering Nelios's intransigence as recently as lunchtime, she winced. 'Can I suggest you speak to Nelios first before you come?'

'Speak to me about what?' came the query.

She spun round to see him entering the room, Angelos tucked snugly against his chest. The sight of father and son sent another pulse of yearning through her. Which was absurd, because this was exactly what she'd agreed to, so why the further yearning...

Her breath caught as realisation deepened. *She wanted more*.

'Vayle?'

'Agnes wants to come to Athens.'

She watched his gaze shift to the screen and saw myriad expressions flicker over his chiselled features before his eyes swung back to her and stayed for an eternity.

'I would like to spend some time alone with my wife and son. When I'm ready to talk, I'll send my plane for you. Is that agreeable?' he said with very little give.

Agnes's eyes widened before she nodded eagerly. 'Y-yes. *Efkharisto*.'

His gaze was still locked on Vayle. 'I was going to show Angelos the sunset. Join us when you're done.'

She was sure he hadn't meant it as an order, despite it sounding like that. Because they'd just enjoyed a pleasant, non-confrontational few hours, and an invitation to watch the sunset shouldn't be an order. She and Agnes spoke for a few more minutes, then she hung up.

The sun was showing off when she stepped out to join them on the terrace. Deep orange flirted with slashes of yellow and red, but she stopped for a moment to take in the more striking sight of her baby cradled in Nelios's arms.

'Come here or you'll miss it,' he drawled without turning round.

Edging closer, she glanced at his face. Tension from minutes ago remained but, when he looked at her, there was no censure in it. It was almost as if he'd already relegated it to the back of his mind until he needed to deal with it.

'Can I look forward to our time on Apeiron free from pressure about Agnes?' he rasped, his eyes returning to the horizon.

Deciding to take a leaf out of his book, she stepped up to the railing and smiled down at Angelos, who had zero interest in the sunset and raptly stared up at his father instead.

'Yes.'

Nelios nodded and, while he was too formidable to show his relief, she sensed it as he gazed down at his son and the corner of his mouth twitched. 'It seems beauty is lost on him. For now at least.'

'Hmm, maybe not entirely,' she murmured before she could stop herself.

His gaze transferred to her, his eyes glinting.

Then, wrapping his free arm around her to draw her closer, they stopped speaking entirely and simply basked in the moment.

Touching is not forbidden.

As glaring slippery slopes went, this one came with flashing neon lights so bright, they might have been seen from space. But could she push the warning away long enough to rationalise it or remember just why not touching Nelios was the safest option? Because *he* seemed to have zero qualms about touching her after their heated kiss in the hotel room.

He touched her back as he guided her onto the plane

bright and early the next morning. And as he offered her a segment of the juicy clementine she'd thought he was peeling for himself right until he held it out to her, his thumb brushing her lower lip when she accepted, heart lurching wildly.

And then there was Angelos's feeding times. Repeatedly Nelios asked if she minded him staying. She always said no, she didn't. She wasn't ashamed of breastfeeding her son in public or wherever his need demanded, so it wasn't what caused the relentless turbulence inside her. It was the possessive hunger in Nelios's eyes, the eagerness to learn everything he could about his son. To record everything, given he'd missed the three months since Angelos was born.

It was as if she'd been given the floor to wax lyrical about her favourite subject on earth to an ardent audience of one. If this was a ploy on his part to gain some sort of leverage in this marriage, then she had to applaud him. He was succeeding hand over fist.

And that was even before the small plane they'd boarded from Italy touched down on a narrow strip of runway on a jewelled island in the middle of the Aegean.

Between what she saw on the internet, her brief jaunt as a stowaway-turned-tourist in Buenos Aires and living in London, one of most cosmopolitan cities on the planet, Vayle thought she couldn't be stunned speechless by anywhere.

She was now. Apeiron was aptly named for its shape that followed an almost perfect infinity sign. The villa followed the outer eastward curve that faced a rolling vista of green bordering white sandy beaches to the pinched middle of the island. The westward curve was much craggier, full of trees, orchards, shallow and steep brown hills and even a tiny church poised on top of a gentle promontory, alongside smaller clusters of villas and a smattering of goats and sheep. It was a place she could see Angelos exploring to his heart's content when he was older.

Altogether, it was less than a kilometre across at its furthest point, but she felt as though it had everything a family needed. A proper family, not one cobbled together by a dozen pieces of paper, signed and witnessed by sharply suited men in a hotel room. That squeeze in her chest signalling the ever-deepening yearning arrived and stayed all through the tour, Nelios escorting them to the fully decked-out nursery that held everything a treasured baby boy would need.

'Is this all right?' Nelios asked, his rapt gaze flicking between his son and her.

Her heart full, Vayle nodded. 'More than. Thank you.' And, if there was the shadow of a crumb of envy that yearned for some of that attention, well, she kept that disgraceful notion to herself.

She spun away to eye the two doors leading off opposite sides of the nursery.

'They're adjoining suites. Mine is through there. And this is yours. We can both check on Angelos when needed.'

Walking forward as he spoke, he threw open the doors leading to her suite…and stunned her all over again. There was a probability that one day she might get blasé about the luxury Nelios seemed to take in his stride. Today wasn't that day.

But you have nearly two decades to get used to it. Her heart didn't jump at the thought. But that squeezing replayed, harder, more insistent than before.

'We share a common terrace,' he went on, watching her with an edgy ferocity, as if it was vitally important to him that he interpret what she felt. Spotting a snazzy baby's rocking chair similar to one they'd used before placed under a large sun umbrella complete with a light blanket, Vayle placed a drowsy Angelos in it and strapped him in. His eyes were drooping even before she turned away and walked to the edge of the terrace where Nelios was staring at the horizon. While the atmosphere was a little charged—and she suspected that, for as long as they were in close proximity, that chemistry they'd both acknowledged would create its own ecosystem—there was a lack of prowling restlessness about it.

It was as if Nelios was at peace here. 'You didn't just name this place for its shape, did you?'

He paused for a second, then sent her a tight smile. 'I had an awakening of sorts here. The previous owner, who was forced to leave for health reasons, didn't want to sell to me at first. Not until I'd given him a vision of what my intentions were for his pride and joy.'

'I'm guessing he didn't want it turned into a hedonistic Club Med destination for the rich?'

His mouth quirked. 'Exactly so. And he wasn't impressed with the prospect of another Nelios hotel, no matter how selective the clientele, or how sympathetic to the environment I intended to be.'

'What was the awakening?'

'That only my life was finite. That what I left behind could be truly infinite.' His gaze drifted to his sleeping son. 'I saw it as leaving a legacy without having actual offspring, but now I'm seeing it's even better with.'

'And that's all it took to sway him?'

He shook his head and a guarded look descended over his face. 'No. I told him that, for every year I owned his island, I would fund a necessary project somewhere in the world.'

Her eyes widened. 'Really?'

'*Ne.*' His gaze paused in the middle distance for an age before he glanced at her. 'That morning after our night in Buenos Aires, I left because I had to oversee one of those projects.' His shoulder twitched. 'Granted, I didn't have to leave that early, but I still would've left.'

She filed away the confession and pushed to satisfy her curiosity. 'What was the project?'

'Five hundred homes for families who need to relocate from the slums. Another five hundred for struggling families with young children who are at risk of being made homeless—or worse.'

Families, children, his possessive claiming of Angelos: she didn't need a crystal ball to show her that, while Nelios was a wildly successful tycoon, there was an equally resolute part of him that was obsessed with righting the wrongs done to him at whatever level he could achieve. He couldn't see that, in obsessing over the past, he was adversely affecting his present…and his future too.

Knowing she risked shattering the relative peace and tranquillity, she licked her lips and pushed ahead anyway. 'You still owe me a re-telling of your story.'

He stiffened and his jaw worked for a few tense seconds. But the furious rejection never arrived. He remained tense but slowly his jaw unclenched, as did the bunched fists resting on the stone balustrade.

After a minute of his gaze roving the landscape, he finally spoke. 'I told you the foster carer judged me as a problem child on that first day she visited?'

Her nod was jerky, her emotions churning with distress for him. 'Yes.'

He shrugged. 'In the first month alone, I ended up being moved to three different foster homes, each one progressively worse than the last.'

Her heart squeezed tighter when he exhaled harshly.

'In the third month, I was placed with carers who believed the harsher the corporal punishment they doled out, the better.' Naked fury washed over his face and she knew he was reliving the horrendous memory. 'It didn't matter how young or old the children were. They all received the same treatment—a fist or a belt for the smallest infraction.'

'God.'

His head jerked down, his mouth thinning. 'I grew tired of it very quickly. Especially when it became clear they weren't beating us just to be corrective but to merely suppress us because they could. It was base cruelty for the sake of it, because they could get away with and it and be rewarded with a pay cheque at the end of the month. So I decided to do something about it.'

Her eyes widened. 'What did you do?'

'My first instinct was just to leave. I figured the streets would be far better than what I was enduring.' The harsh twist of his mouth suggested he'd discovered differently. 'But I couldn't leave the other children under those conditions, especially the three younger ones.'

Her little finger bumped his and she realised she'd moved closer without conscious thought. He glanced down at where they touched for a long moment before his gaze returned to the horizon.

'By a stroke of fate, luck or whatever you wish to call it, the decision was taken out of my hands. A lit cigarette left untended by a drunk foster mother literally ignited the start I wanted.'

'Your foster home went up in flames?'

He nodded. 'Down to the last cinder. I got the kids out and waited until the fire brigade and ambulance arrived to take care of them. Then I put my plan in place and took my chances on the streets.'

If her chest had been tight before, it barely let her breathe now. Tears stung the back of her eyes. 'That wasn't a breeze, though, was it?' she murmured.

'Far from it. And especially not when I discovered I wasn't alone.'

She blinked. 'What?'

His mouth twitched. 'Turns out another kid had the same idea.'

'Andreas?' she guessed.

He shook his head. 'Capaldi. He'd followed me. So I was a thirteen-year-old in charge of a ten-year-old on the streets of Athens.'

Her heart leapt into her throat. She glanced back at her peacefully sleeping son, dying inside at the horror of imagining him ten years from now suffering what Capaldi had. And when her hand moved to cover his it was a conscious effort of empathy and encouragement. 'How did you manage to…survive?'

'By the skin of our teeth,' he rasped. 'And sometimes with borrowed fortitude.'

'Is that…when you met Andreas?'

He jerked out a nod. 'On the very night when I believed my luck had run out. We were cornered in an alley with a gang who believed we were trespassing on their territory. Andreas happened to be hiding in the same alley. And he, it turned out, had more experience with gang warfare than I did.' He didn't elaborate and she didn't ask. He'd previously told her that Andreas's story was his to tell if he wished, but she got the awful gist of it.

They remained in sombre silence for several minutes until she drew in a shaky breath. 'What you said to me before, about my father's flaws not being mine... You know that applies to you too, right?'

The corners of his mouth turned down but he remained in stoic, rigid silence. It felt essential that she try to get through to him. To break through the fortress of bitterness he'd built around himself.

'Look around you, Nelios. See how far you've come. You've risen above the worst things thrown at you and triumphed. Don't you think it's time to let that little boy go?'

His smile was humourless. He didn't follow her gaze, didn't take in the evidence of all he'd achieved. If anything his face grew more sombre, more resolute. 'That's where you're wrong. I don't intend to ever let that little boy go. He's the motivation that fuels me to remember what human beings are really capable of. How utterly despicable they can be.'

'But keeping such a tight grip on the past means you can't reach for a better future. Don't you see?' Again, the sense of urgency throbbing within her said she was pushing not just for him but for herself and Angelos too.

He glanced down at her, the blind fury in his eyes telling her he didn't hear; that he was locked in that very same past. Several seconds passed before he controlled it. 'Do you know, I kept track of those last foster parents? And, the second they found themselves a new hovel, they tried to round up the kids they'd endangered again. I made sure they never fostered again.'

'How?'

His smile was filled with satisfied vengeance. 'Turns out if you bombard a certain helpline with stories of abuse, even the laziest social worker eventually gets off their ass to do something.'

'This just proves my point. You've done so much for

others. Don't you owe it to yourself to take that next step and put your past to rest?'

His jaw clenched tight in resolute mutiny.

She sighed. 'Then you'll never leave that alley. Never truly find peace. Is that what you really want?'

He snapped his gaze from hers and returned it to the glittering sea. 'What I want is answers. And so I guess I should thank you for facilitating that.'

'Once Agnes gives you all the answers you need? Then what?'

Another macabre smile etched his face for a single moment before it was gone. 'Then I'll use it as fuel to ensure I'm by far a better parent than they ever were. Then I will be vindicated for cutting them out of my life. I moved on a long time ago, Vayle. This will just confirm I was right to do so. But moving on doesn't mean the broken parts of me will eventually be fixed. It's too late for that. Sorry to burst your little bubble, but that's never going to happen.'

Shock rocked through her, keeping her rooted to the spot as he turned and walked away. Far from believing she was breaking through to him, it seemed Nelios didn't intend to budge an iota, despite his clear pain. So, while her every instinct screamed at her to follow him, to keep battering at the fortress, her head overruled it. Nelios was deeply entrenched in his ways and beliefs. One conversation wasn't going to overcome that.

If she had the time and patience, and it seemed she had eighteen years of it, then what was the hurry?

She turned from the blissful view and padded over to pick up her son. Hugging him close, smelling his baby scent, she told herself that, no, there was no hurry, even if that clock inside her whispered that time might not be the tool she needed in this endeavour.

That she might need…something else.
Something *riskier*.

If Nelios had expected an unhappy wife at the dinner table when he walked into his dining room after hours of steaming away in his study with an unhealthy amount of righteous indignation, he was mistaken. Pleasantly mistaken—perhaps that even unsettled him.

There was no hint in her manner that him walking away from her, after practically criticising her for bothering to find the silver lining in the cloud of his past trauma, had upset her. He knew his intractability hadn't sat well with her if the dull light in her eyes had been any indication.

He nearly tripped over his own feet when she looked up…and smiled. Not the blindingly fake one some women used to express their rabid glee to be in his presence. Not the batting-eyelashes one that said a request for a favour lurked just beneath the surface. It was heart stopping, groin stirring—not that he needed help for that to happen. Not when she looked more breathtaking each time he saw her.

And with that smile… He sucked in a slow, control-restoring breath, which failed miserably.

She wore a white halter-neck dress threaded with gold that seemed to reflect off her smooth skin. Her hair was down in gorgeous waves around her shoulders and those hoop earrings that had driven him insane in Buenos Aires were on show once more. Her perfume, floral and exquisite, called to him and it felt positively sinful not to bend and place a kiss on her cheek. Or on that gentle slope of her shoulder. So that was exactly what he did.

'If it's not against your infernal rules, can I say how beautiful you look?' he said when he lifted his head.

Her smile remained in place but a breathless quality to

her breathing surged pleasure through him, increasing the pressure in his groin.

Her teeth toyed with her lower lip and she tucked a strand of hair over her ear before shrugging. 'I'll allow it.'

It was absurd that something eased inside him then, as if he'd been on tenterhooks, when he was his own man and had earned the right not to need to placate anyone. *Especially* when he was in the right. *'Efkharisto,'* he drawled as he sat down and shook out his napkin.

Equally disturbing—and the reason he'd spent hours staring into space when he was supposed to have been working—was that the decades-old weight he'd carried seemed somehow...lighter. A realisation that logic insisted had something to do with unburdening himself to Vayle.

But, now they were back on an even keel, he didn't need to think about it any more. They were done with the quid pro quo of trauma-sharing. Now they could move onto better things.

She asked about his other humanitarian projects and he gladly told her about the one-thousand-strong children's charity in Panama, the bird sanctuary in Lithuania and the children's education funds in a dozen countries. And, dearest to his heart, the camps for orphans and street kids right here in Greece, ably managed by Capaldi's wife.

'I'm not sure why I'm so stunned he's married with kids. He seems so...' Vayle's voice trailed off.

'Fearsome?' he offered with a hint of a smile—another thing he was doing more and more around her. 'It's a prerequisite for working for me.'

She rolled her eyes as she smiled and, *thee mou*, he wanted to kiss that mouth more than he wanted his next breath.

Which made the words that came out of his mouth as

they were enjoying coffee and dessert quite absurd. Because even he knew he was skirting the volcanic rim of temptation. 'We'll take the boat out tomorrow—explore the island some more, *ne*?'

She nodded, and her hair slid over her skin in a silken curtain he wanted to run through his fingers so badly, he had to curl them around his coffee cup to stall the impulse.

'Sounds good.'

And so their surprisingly delightful evening went, followed by a nightcap in the salon and half an hour of television, until a wide yawn from her had him surging to his feet, his hand held out.

She blinked, a little warily, perhaps also fighting off the charged mood that hovered far too close. But she rose, put her hand in his and let him walk her to their suite door.

Together they checked on their son then, in tones echoing the unnerving yearning he didn't want to voice, he wished her *kalinikta*. He watched her blink again before nodding, then she disappeared behind her own doors.

Leaving him standing there—a little shaken, a lot stunned. Because it seemed, in just under seventy-two hours, his wife had slid so effectively under his skin, and he would be so very hard pressed ever to remove her.

And he wasn't entirely sure he wanted to.

CHAPTER NINE

'I THINK YOU either need a dictionary or a pair of prescription glasses. Because that is definitely not a boat.'

Vayle looked from the massive vessel growing bigger as they neared it to the mildly amused man sitting at the helm of the tender. Nelios shrugged. The heart that'd expanded then wedged itself hard against her ribcage when he'd knocked on her door after breakfast in a pair of designer shorts and a white T-shirt raced harder as her gaze moved over him.

Surprisingly, she'd gone to bed with a smile on her face and had slept sounder than she had in years, rising to feed Angelos before topping off her sleep and waking up delightfully refreshed.

'It's a floating device that suits our purposes for the day.'

She snorted. 'A floating device is a dinghy. This is a…a…' She shook her head, unable to locate an accurate descriptive for the immense super-yacht in front of them.

It was gorgeous, granted, as was everything Nelios owned. And it resembled a small floating city. As they rounded it, she caught glimpses of jet skis, swimming pools, sun-lounging decks and even a helipad—all the bells and whistles a billionaire could want.

'Are you finally rendered speechless, *yineka mou*?'

My wife. This particular endearment secretly thrilled her. As did the careful way he lifted Angelos's portable cradle, then turned to hold his hand out to her to help her off the launch. It didn't matter that half a dozen staff and crew waited to assist them. It made Vayle feel special. Which made the yearning deepen into a wish for...more.

She bit her lip as she followed him on board the super-yacht, then up a flight of stairs onto the first of many sun-splashed decks. They had a long day ahead of them. And the little scheme she'd concocted bubbled all sorts of warnings at the back of her head as the hours passed.

Nelios slanted her increasingly frequent looks as they swam, lunched and played with Angelos, telling her she wasn't hiding her nerves very well.

'What's going on in that mind of yours?' he drawled after returning from putting Angelos down for his afternoon nap. 'You've been jumpier than a hot bean in the last hour.'

He handed her a fresh glass of fruit punch and helped himself to mineral water. When he raised the sunscreen bottle, she swallowed and nodded, watching him walk in a loose-limbed, drop-dead hot prowl towards where she stood against the railing.

They were anchored just off their private beach, on the widest deck of the super-yacht, surrounded by loungers, a bar and a pool for when it got too hot and they wanted a dip. They'd circled Apeiron earlier and he'd pointed out the various places for diving, snorkelling and which beach was the best for all-day sun.

She bit her lip, wondering how best to phrase her crazy idea. In the end, it came tumbling out. 'I want to amend our rule. Not break it entirely, just...tweak it a little.'

He stilled behind her, the hand with which he'd been

about to apply the lotion hovering an inch from her shoulder. Staring up at him, Vayle couldn't tell how he felt about that, his face a carefully neutral mask.

'In what way, specifically?' he intoned then, low and deep. His voice had taken on that timbre ever since she'd dropped her white beach kaftan to reveal the burnished orange bikini she wore underneath. The pre-wedding spa pampering her wedding coordinator had insisted on, and the pockets of sunshine she'd enjoyed since Italy, had added a warm glow to her skin. And her secret thrill had increased after seeing Nelios couldn't take his eyes off her.

When both hands slid down the slopes of her neck to circle lotion into her shoulders, it made it easier for her to say a little more vehemently than she'd intended, 'I don't want to completely change the "no sex" part.' An assertion that didn't go unnoticed when his eyes narrowed and the hands gliding down her spine paused just above her bottom before reversing their journey up her spine.

'Are you attempting to convince me you didn't enjoy sex with me?' he asked silkily, with more than a hint of mocking disbelief laced in there.

'Not at all,' she hurried to say, the effect of his hands on her making her voice husky and many parts of her body tingle and unfurl and dampen. 'On the contrary, I enjoyed it a little too much. Which is why I'm still advocating abstaining, but with a small amendment.'

'That doesn't make any sense, *agapiméni*,' he stated indolently.

'Does it not? I'm told liquid morphine and sky-diving are some of the best highs ever to grace this earth. But do you see me hankering after either of them?'

His breath seemed to stall. Then he caught her elbow and

turned her round so he could start on her arms. Those done, he dropped to a crouch in front of her and began on her legs.

And once he had one foot propped on his knee, applying sunscreen in slow, spine-melting strokes, he glanced up at her with hooded eyes. 'Are you saying you fear an addiction to me, *glikia mou*?'

Well...she'd stepped right into that one, hadn't she? She tried to shrug her way out of it. 'An addiction to the act—not you. There's a difference.'

His nostrils flared. 'I fail to see how there is. And you should think carefully before you suggest sex with another man will be the same as with me. Because, for one thing, you will never get the chance to find out.'

Since the very thought of it made her skin crawl, and she didn't see the point in aggravating him any more, she waved him away. 'My point is, you should be pleased I'm troubleshooting this problem before it gets us both in trouble.'

'Speak for yourself. I'm extremely adept at self-control.'

That he took vast pleasure in informing her of that, riled her. It made her immediately want to put that titanium control to the test, even if it was to teach him a lesson.

Before she could talk herself out of it, she was unhooking the clasp of her bikini top. Letting it loosen, she pulled it off and tossed it away.

He stiffened, his nostrils flaring wide before pinching in a sharply drawn breath. 'Vayle, what the hell are you doing?' His voice was oiled gravel, grinding desire into her bloodstream.

'What does it look like? I'm testing your famous control, of course.' Last night she'd convinced herself making Nelios snap was the best way to kick down if not all of his guard, at least some of it. Enough so she could push through to him, make him see past what he thought was broken to consider a different perspective. One that included him… *them*…having a semblance of a pain-free life. One in which she wouldn't be so terrified to admit what her heart was telling her—that she felt more for him than was anywhere near wise, even if she wasn't going to back away from that revelation. Yet—unless she knew all hope was gone.

She'd taken a chance once and opened her heart to affection when she could've remained mired in bitterness from her father's rejection. And she'd found a family who'd cared for her. Maybe lightning would strike twice. If she was brave enough to let it?

His head whipped about, even though his staff knew better than to interrupt them. When he was satisfied there were no prying eyes, his scorching gaze returned to her. His laziness evaporated as he slowly surged from his crouch, his eyes fixed squarely on her chest as he tossed the sunscreen lotion aside and braced his hands on either side of her, caging her in.

'And how do you mean to do that?' he rasped.

Good question. Now she was half-naked and burning with the inferno in his eyes, she seriously questioned what she was doing. But the thought of backing down, of scooping up her top and retreating, rubbed her the wrong way.

So she did the opposite. She stepped forward, cocked her hip and revelled in the rapt zeal in his eyes when he followed the movement. 'To see which one of us breaks first, without the final act.'

Oh, God. Really? Was she insane?

'Are you insane?' he echoed.

She thought she must be, because his query only spurred her on. 'If you don't want this, just call uncle.'

'Absolutely not.'

She licked her lips, stifling a moan when his dark eyes hungrily followed her tongue. 'Well, then…'

'Are there rules to this dangerous game you're playing or are you making it up on the fly?'

Her eyes dropped to the T-shirt stretching across his chiselled chest. 'You're allowed to take one item of clothing off too.'

The words were barely out of his mouth before he ripped the shirt over his head and tossed it away, leaving her with a view that rivalled what lay beyond the yacht. A view that made her nipples bud painfully; made his sensual lips curve with pure vainglory.

'What next, *yineka mou*?' Gravel had turned to a silken web he was using to entice and enthral. And when he sprawled back to his original position, supremely confident he had regained the upper hand, she fought not to grit her teeth. Or call uncle herself.

'One kiss—no hands. Who breaks or retreats first loses.'

An unholy light gleamed in his eyes for a distressing stretch, during which she questioned her judgement once again and almost prayed he would say *hell, no* and back out.

But, damn it, on top of this insanity cake she'd baked for herself now sat the exquisite promise of the cherry of kissing Nelios once more. An act she hadn't quite allowed herself to admit she'd missed desperately until this second.

So when he slowly walked back without taking his eyes off her, sat down on the nearest sofa and patted his thighs with two hard slaps of invitation, she stopped herself from the visibly vulnerable act of swallowing. She hastened to close the distance, dropped a knee on either side of his thighs, then grasped the top of the seat. The small win of seeing him swallow instead didn't last very long when he leaned forward immediately and brought his mouth *dan-*

gerously close to hers, leaving it right there...tantalisingly just out of reach.

'If you want me, come and get me,' he taunted, rough and undaunted.

She withstood the bait...barely. But she countered by arching her back, dragging her naked chest over his and letting him feel the warm peaks of her nipples.

His hands clenched at his side. 'Fuck,' he muttered under his breath.

She continued the figure-eight roll, almost losing her rhythm when she felt the power of his arousal between her legs—a little salty, a little musky but all rampant, raw man.

She nibbled along his jaw to his ear, then caught his lobe between her teeth, smiling when a shudder coursed through him. But then the fine hairs on his chest whispered across her nipples and she was shuddering and jerking in his lap. Vayle felt her core dampen and prayed he would mistake it for being the result of her dip in the ocean.

But then he inhaled greedily. 'You smell incredible, *eros mou*,' he praised gutturally.

She squeezed her eyes shut, just to gather her fraying composure. 'Thank you.'

Then she sealed her mouth to his, letting free the moan trapped inside her for an eternity. She'd barely tasted him before he took control, swiping her mouth open with his tongue and diving in to tangle and conquer hers. Need drove her to gyrate on top of him, dragging her nipples across his chest to alleviate their ache. But all it did was build and build the tension and scream at her to quench her thirst. Their kiss turned increasingly frenzied, Nelios biting, laving, coaxing then cursing when it didn't feel like enough; when every second poured further fuel on the fire.

The urge to throw in the towel arrived like a lightning

strike. Before she could act on it, firm hands grasped her waist and Nelios set her aside with jerky movements. He shot to his feet, his fingers ploughing through his hair. When his hands dropped, they clenched and unclenched, then he stalked over to the drinks cabinet and poured a shot of cognac as she hurriedly tugged on her bikini top.

After he downed the drink, he spun round. 'Enough. We will call it a draw. This time.'

Vayle shook her head, face flaming and trembling with unsatisfied need. 'There won't be a next time. I…shouldn't have done that. It was reckless.'

His eyes darkened. 'Or it simply proved that you shouldn't have implemented that no-sex clause and I certainly shouldn't have accepted it. Not when our chemistry is this volatile. It'll only lead to other incidents like this, inevitably.'

Hot denial rose, then died on the tip of her tongue. Because even now the brutal withdrawal her body was going through went beyond shaming her. It laid bare the truth he'd stated. They were weak when it came to one another. Games, challenges and denials would get them nowhere. Looking to shatter his control and meeting resistance while laying herself bare would only lead to turmoil.

He exhaled harshly and her gaze latched onto him, a slave to her need. The imprint of his erection made her stifle a moan.

'Nelios…'

'I don't know about you, but I need a cold shower—right now. The ball remains in your court. But know that, if you find your way to my bed, this time I will not be setting you free any time soon.'

With that mike drop, he walked off, his long strides carrying him away before she'd drawn the shuddering breath which did zip to calm her.

* * *

She managed, barely, to throttle her need until it was a manageable bubble lodged deep inside her for the rest of the day.

Whether Nelios's control was back in place, she couldn't quite tell. She felt his heated gaze often, but every time she glanced his way his expression was either shuttered or fixed on their son. Conversation flowed calmly during dinner and on their return home, but when they said goodnight she wondered, *feared*, if she'd only made things worse.

It was a relief to be awakened by Angelos for his nighttime feed. But she'd only just placed him on her breast when the door to Nelios's bedroom opened and he walked out.

'Oh, you're up. There's no need for you to be... I mean, I'm okay with...' She stumbled to a halt, hiding a grimace.

He smiled a crooked smile, then slotted the snazzy little baby monitor into his pocket. The act pulled down his silk pyjama bottoms a little, displaying the chiselled line of muscle that framed his pelvis so gloriously.

Feeling that bubble expand, Vayle dragged her gaze away, concentrating on Angelos, who was already being lulled back into a milk coma. When they'd first arrived here and she'd seen his nursery, she'd wondered why there were two arm chairs. Watching Nelios sink into one with every intention of sticking around, she got it.

He shrugged one bare, deliciously muscled shoulder. 'You have to be up, for obvious reasons. But there's no reason to do it alone.'

There was a time when she'd called this man a monster. No longer. With each considerate act, he was burrowing into her vulnerable places.

And she felt inclined to...let him. Especially when he continued to watch her with that hungry fascination she suspected he wasn't fully aware was on display.

He stayed until Angelos had fallen asleep again. Stayed at her side as she placed him in his cot and drew his blanket over him. Stayed to drop a kiss on his son's head. Then, with a heavy-lidded look, he bade her goodnight and retreated as silently as he'd arrived.

Leaving her staring at his closed door, her heart racing madly.

She felt inclined to...let him.

It might have been seconds, or an hour. But, with a compulsion she couldn't deny, Vayle found herself standing before his door, her hand shaking as she reached for the handle that might not be locked against her after all. She squeezed her eyes shut for a second, then opened them. She turned the handle and nudged open the door open.

He wasn't asleep but sitting up in bed, as she'd half-suspected he would be. His gaze founds hers immediately, as if he'd been waiting for her.

'Come to test my peace of mind once more, to drive me out of it, or is it something else?'

She couldn't speak past her overpowering need so she shook her head.

'You'll need to speak the words, Vayle. So there's no equivocation or misunderstanding.'

Her mouth dried. She couldn't very well say she wanted to reach his heart through sex; that would be too exposing. And being here, right now, felt exposing enough. 'I...' She paused, her heart hammering loud enough to fill her ears with a thunderous roar. 'I need you.' That would have to be enough, she adjudged.

And if that was a glint of disappointment in his eyes, he hid it well by veiling them with his long lashes, tossing back his sheets and ordering her to, 'Come here, *yineka mou*.'

She went. Hell, she *stumbled*. He caught her easily, expertly, and before she could draw another breath flipped her beneath him, pinning her to the bed with his powerful body. Staring down at her with a predatory gaze.

'You agree that attempting to drive us both to the brink of insanity, only to withdraw, was an exercise that was always going to fail, yes?'

Her nails bit into his shoulders in protest and in irritation that, yet again, he'd been right. 'Yes! Fine, it was a ridiculous thing to do. Are you happy now?'

'Not yet. But I'm getting there. Now, spread your legs for your husband. Let me taste you, *omorfi mou*.'

He devoured her with a confidence-stroking hunger that bordered on frightening, it was so heady. And she let her delight show freely, vocalising, touching and stroking with abandon.

'*Thee mou*,' he muttered. 'You really throw yourself into your passions, don't you?'

'Are you complaining?'

'Absolutely not.' He took her hand and dragged it to his groin, his eyes blazing into hers as he wrapped both sets of their fingers around his sizeable girth. 'Does this feel like a complaint to you, *eros mou*?'

'N-no.'

He smiled, looking a little pained, infinitely hot. Until she stroked him. Then a different look etched his face. 'Fuck!'

'Yes. Please. I want you.'

Her fervent whisper transformed him. Transported him to a higher plane. Between one heartbeat and the next, he'd tugged on a condom and her flimsy lace and silk was a useless tangle on the floor.

'I will take it slow next time. Worship you as you deserve. But you will admit you've driven me to the brink, wife?'

'Yes, worship later. Need you…now.'

Her grasping hands reached for him, and she loved it when he leaned down over her, then moved her onto her side. Slotting in behind her, he pulled her hip into his, holding her steady with one hand.

With the other speared into her hair, eyes as rich and dark as the cosmos at night, Nelios surged into her. His groan synced with her scream, a private, decadent symphony of lust and pleasure never before experienced by her. And, from the words that fell from his lips, she would wager a great deal that it was unique for him too.

'Vayle… Vayle… You feel…so good.'

'Don't stop. Please don't stop,' she begged hoarsely, her fingers scrambling back to clutch him any way she could, ensnare him in this divine space with her.

'Impossible,' he growled, his voice barely coherent.

When the hand on her hip moved to circle her waist to trap her harder against him, she felt her throat clog, tears springing to sting her eyes. She was thankful for the former, because it prevented her from pleading for him never to let her go. To want her beyond what a piece of paper decreed. Even beyond what this insane chemistry had thrust upon them.

Instead, she squeezed her eyes shut and surrendered to the majesty of making love with Nelios. She didn't even care when he wrecked her by keeping her poised on the edge of climax for an eternity before, with a guttural command to, 'Open your eyes for me, *eros mou*. Show me your desire,' he kept her waiting for another sublime minute before diving with her off the cliff into a sea of pleasure so pure, she knew in her soul it was changing her for ever.

Realigning her very existence in ways she might never recover from.

* * *

The days that followed blurred into a golden haze, each moment so exquisitely saturated with bliss it bordered on the surreal. Their impromptu honeymoon unfolded like a fantasy spun from silk and starlight, each hour with Nelios a heady mix of seduction and serenity that lodged itself deep beneath her skin.

He made her laugh—deep, unguarded laughter that burst free before she could stop it—then kissed her until the world fell away, until fear and caution melted like sugar on her tongue. Until she couldn't remember what she'd ever needed protecting from.

He was present at each feed of Angelos. And in the mornings, she woke tangled in heat, scent and masculine strength, his arm heavy across her waist, his breath a whisper against her nape. His touch—possessive even in sleep—anchoring her in a reality that felt too good to be true.

And that was the danger, wasn't it? Because, in those precious moments between night and day, when dreams lingered and reality hadn't yet sharpened its claws, she let herself imagine that this was real. That this wasn't just chemistry or obligation dressed in silk sheets and sun-drenched kisses. That maybe—just maybe—he felt it too.

But always, without fail, reality slid in on quiet feet. In the way his gaze sometimes drifted, shadowed and unreadable. In the way his silences occasionally stretched too long, heavy with words he refused to say, more often than not after her conversations with Agnes. But she told herself that, as much as it hurt to watch him retreat to that fortress with no drawbridge, she wasn't about to neglect her contact with Agnes to please him.

Unfortunately, the tension was what kept her heart in limbo. The clause they'd so spectacularly broken had been her last defence, the final line between falling and freefall. And she'd leapt, willingly, into his arms.

Yet, as the blissful weeks turned into a month, then closer to two, it was less a soaring through ecstasy and more like plummeting straight towards heartbreak.

Because, as soul-searing as it was, this had never just been about sex—not for her. It was *him*. The man who held her at night as if she was the only thing tethering him to the earth. The man whose past stood between them like the Great Wall.

So, even as they danced barefoot on moon-washed sands, she held part of herself back. She clung to hope desperately, even as it slipped through her fingers.

Because fairy tales weren't meant to last.

Were they?

CHAPTER TEN

NELIOS SAT ON the beach, arms resting on his knees, watching the sun rise and the waves crash from the sea he'd just swum in.

For a man neck-deep in the most pleasurable weeks of his life, his gut churned far too agitatedly for his liking. It was what had driven him from his bed when he should be wrapped around his wife.

But... The feeling of time running out wouldn't leave him.

In all the years he'd thought of the parents who'd abandoned him, he'd never been this riled up *emotionally*. Sure, there'd been much fury and bitterness, as was his right. But it'd been ruthlessly overlaid with icy, implacable resolve. And, once he'd divorced himself from the past and got down to the very real business of surviving, he'd locked any superfluous emotions away.

Yes, they'd been ruffled when he'd come face-to-face with his mother and tangled with Vayle and her last year. But control had soon reasserted itself, as it so often did, when he'd won and then triumphantly walked away.

He didn't feel so much in control now. The growing emotions he didn't really want to label as nerves and...*panic*...

but couldn't see any other way to describe them, tunnelled a different path through him.

The past weeks had been blissful—another term that greatly alarmed him, but admittedly in a good way. Vayle had come to him and they'd obliterated that terrible clause that would've made them both suffer unnecessarily. And, boy, had they taken advantage of it since then.

He'd enjoyed his wife anywhere and everywhere all over Apeiron, delighting in showing her different sexual experiences that left a deep flush on her cheeks and stars in her eyes.

As for him... Having been intent on eradicating any emotional fallout from the women he'd tangled with in the past, he'd never slept with the same woman for this long before. It was...novel, pleasurable. Satisfying, even.

He knew enough to know he didn't want to upset that particular apple cart. He didn't want Vayle upset. But also enough to know a giant spanner was heading into what had become a smooth operation.

You know the root cause of this situation—how to fix it.

He shifted and rolled onto his feet, impatient with the persistent voice. Then with the far too beautiful view that taunted him with its perfection, highlighting that his life was far from perfect.

Vayle's admonishments about the consequences of living in the past rang in his ears. His thoughts were so busy crowding each other, he didn't realise he'd walked all the way to his suite until she turned from viewing the sunrise on their terrace.

'Hey, you were gone when I woke up. Are you okay?' she murmured softly, examining his face in that way she had that made him think she could see his every bitter— perhaps irredeemable—thought. That all this examining and hedging was if not now, then soon to be the very thing that wrote him off in her eyes.

'No need to worry about me, *glikia mou*.'

There was a defensive bite in there that made him shift again, annoyed when he saw his glib remark hadn't quite done the trick of reassuring her. Silence stretched just a little too long. He knew her well enough by now to recognize the slight tightening of her shoulders, the way she absently traced the lip of the coffee cup in her hand.

She was winding up to tell him something. He didn't look at her. He didn't have to.

'Agnes called again,' she said, voice low.

A muscle flexed in his jaw. He froze. Not visibly, not enough for anyone else to notice—but she would. She always did.

'She left a message,' she continued, careful now. 'She's in Athens. She wants to see you.'

He finally turned his head and met her gaze.

'You should call her back,' she pushed.

'No.' The word cracked out of him, too sharply, too desperately. The slipping sensation intensified.

She inhaled slowly, and he could feel her fighting to keep the peace. To keep this moment from detonating. 'Nelios… we had an agreement.'

'And I believe I said I would talk to her, but in my own time.'

She was quiet for a beat. 'If not now, then when?'

Her words curled around something deep inside him, something old, scarred and better left buried. Only it wasn't. She was raking it raw.

'Why does this matter to you so much?' he seethed.

'Because I see what it's doing to you,' she said. There was no accusation, no pleading—just truth; soft, dangerous truth. 'The way you lock parts of yourself away. The way you flinch from your past like it might still reach for you. She's your mother, Nelios.'

His laugh felt acid-sharp. 'She hasn't been. Not for a very long time.'

'Then ask her why. Because if you don't...'

Something sliced deeper, sharper than a scalpel. The panic spurted, then gushed. He clenched his belly tight. 'Be very careful what you say next, *glikia mou*.'

Her gaze lingered on the horizon for a beat, then two, then returned to his. 'Maybe today is a day to be completely reckless.' She folded her arms around herself—a shield. 'I'm not trying to fix you, Nelios. I just want you to stop pretending you're happy dwelling in the past when you're not. You're still bleeding somewhere beneath the surface, and at some point it'll be too late.'

He rose, an instinctual move. He hated looking up at her when he was cornered like this. Hated even more the flicker of guilt in her eyes—because it mirrored the feeling inside him.

'Have at it, if you insist. But you'll be participating on your own,' he said tightly. Then he turned, striding away from her.

'Nelios!'

He didn't stop. But each step dragged something heavy behind it. And, even though he didn't look back, he felt the precise moment his time dwindled to zero in the silence he left behind.

She stood there long after he left.

The terrace felt colder now, as if the sea breeze had turned on her too. A single tear slipped down her cheek—not dramatic, not even bitter, just inevitable.

She lowered herself back into the chair, arms wrapped around her ribs, as if she could hold the crack in her chest closed with sheer will.

He'd walked away from her.

After the past weeks, despite knowing that harsh reality was waiting to pounce, that hurt more than anything else ever could. It was time to accept that Nelios would keep guarding his pain as if it was the only thing that made him who he was. She'd seen the shadows in his eyes when he thought she wasn't looking. Felt the tension in his body when her fingers brushed too close to his heart. Too close to the fortress he'd spent decades building and lovingly tending.

But love—real love—couldn't survive in the dark.

And definitely not the love she now accepted that she felt for him. The kind that wanted to dance in the sunlight all day, every day. The kind that came with rainbows shortly after cleansing rain.

If he insisted on keeping that door locked, then maybe it was time to stop knocking.

Unfortunately, putting thought into action wasn't as easy.

For the next week she withstood the frosty silence and heavy censure, broken in the dead of night in bed when Nelios almost unconsciously dragged her into his arms and they fell on each other with almost desperate abandon.

Despite the hollowness of it, she attempted to convince herself that maybe sex was the stepping stone to this marriage of convenience, based on a piece of paper she didn't want. Vayle suspected it was that abiding demonstration of care and affection for his son that made her own yearning so acute. That made her wish for more, *damn it*.

She wanted Nelios Petralis to throw off the pain from

his past so he could decalcify his heart. *So he could love her.* Because, unless things changed, she was dooming herself to decades of one-sided longing and heartache. Or, she desperately feared, an even quicker exit.

Then a whole new facet to their journey struck.

Her heart swung like a pendulum, one side elation, the other desolation, as she stared down at the test stick in her hand. Despite the care they'd taken, and the fact that she hadn't had her period since Angelos's birth, it seemed somewhere along the line, probably after one of those frantic, middle of the night, half-asleep couplings, nature had taken its course. And lightning had struck twice.

She was pregnant with Nelios's child.

Again.

And, with the bombshell she'd just discovered ticking away furiously beneath her skin, she went in search of Nelios.

To find him packing a bag. 'Wh-where are you going?'

His face was set in forbidding lines she'd hoped never to see again after those hours on his jet that first time. 'To Athens. I have an urgent issue that's arisen there.'

'Were you planning on telling me? Or just sending another of your minions to tell me?'

Was that a wince or was she deluding herself, as she had been about everything?

'I guess we haven't come as far as I thought if common courtesy can fall away so quickly,' she muttered.

'Did you want something, Vayle?'

'Of course. I always want something.' The smile that accompanied her flippant words missed by a mile. 'But alas it seems I'm destined to just want and not get.' She glanced at his case, her heart lurching. 'And I thought you could work from anywhere on earth?' she demanded, her fingers closing around the stick in her pocket.

He stiffened. 'Some meetings are better had in person.'

She frowned, the sense that he wasn't telling the full truth gripping her.

'Nelios—'

'Enough, Vayle. You say you're not trying to fix me, but we both know that's not true, don't we? Because you keep eyeing that can of worms, itching to open it, *ne*? Even though I cannot give you what you want.'

'And what is it that you think I want?'

He looked almost impatient, pained. As if he'd expected her simply to accept that and cower back into her corner. 'What every woman with a ring on her finger seems to want.'

'Security? A roof over her head? Health and happiness for those she cares about? I'm confident I have all of that, thanks to your billions. Or am I missing something?'

He shot her another impatient look. 'You know very well what I'm talking about.'

'And what—you can't bring yourself to say the word? It terrifies you that much?'

His chin jerked as if she'd slapped him. And, while she hoped something had jarred loose, his shuttered expression said he didn't much care for that verbal slap, nor did he intend to alter his thinking. 'You will not taunt me into this.'

'Into what? Into admitting that you're scared to utter the word "love" because you believe it's the Holy Grail destined to be forever denied you? Well, here's a newsflash, Nelios: it's already found you. You mother, our son: they love you. They don't believe it's a flaw to hide from.'

His gaze searched hers with sizzling fervour, searching for something, and for a moment she considered tossing herself onto that pile too, risking it all. But the fear that it might be too harrowing if he rejected her held her tongue.

Already he was retreating. And, as much as she believed she would be strong enough to carry on, eventually, if Nelios Petralis broke her heart, she wouldn't be able to bring herself to walk through that fire.

His jaw gritted. 'Even if that's true, I also believe they're still better off without my brand of...whatever it is that's inside me. The thing that pushed me to take over your hotel, content to make you collateral damage in a war that wasn't even yours to wage.'

She sucked in a shaky breath, then set it free. 'I'll consider forgiving you. You didn't know better. There, that's that taken care of. What next?'

His fingers bunched into fists, so he couldn't reach for things he couldn't have. 'Nothing has changed. Nothing *can* change. I can't risk the freedom of feeling.'

The finality behind the words as he started to walk out shattered her heart. But she couldn't let him have the last word. 'You're so focused on holding onto the prison bars in front of you, you can't see that the doors opened behind you a long time ago. Run, then, if you insist. But I can't promise we'll still be here when you come to your senses.'

Nelios froze, chasing the cycle of emotions on Vayle's face. From hurt to wariness to anger, each one drilled further holes in him.

He wasn't a fool. He could see she wanted more from him. He dragged his gaze from hers, the imploration in her eyes too much to bear. Everything was too damn much. And the more he absorbed the bigger his misfitting parts chafed. He was a broken puzzle, destined always to remain tossed aside in a dusty box. The sooner he accepted that, the better.

Yes, he was better off without that...*love*...anvil-heavy emotion that left a person wide open to the vulnerabilities great and small. When a smile or a frown had the power to turn one's world upside down. It was the sort of weighty responsibility he'd sworn never to fall prey to, even if he could summon such an emotion. Which he couldn't.

As his wife had warned, and Nelios had feared, it was probably already too late. That time on the streets had changed him. And he hadn't exaggerated when he'd told Vayle something was broken inside him. Something that would never let him be free of that frightened little boy who had learned in the most vicious way possible that love was a meaningless construct. A myth tossed about to justify all the anguish and bitterness it had wrought.

But you're not feeling much bitterness any more. And that anguish isn't as terrifying as it used to be, so why don't you—?

He jerked his case off the bed. 'I'm not sure when I'll be back. Maybe a few days. Perhaps a week.'

She shrugged. 'Like I said, take all the time you need. We might be here when you come back, or we might not,' she flung at him.

His insides shredded. Protesting words rose to his lips and one by one they died. He told himself the first lie—that it was better this way.

It wasn't. And the different kind of anguish that filled him was clear evidence of that.

He wasn't even sure why he'd withheld the truth from Vayle—that he was in Athens to speak to his mother.

No. *He knew why.* He'd been...afraid to tell her in case it made no difference, couldn't fix him.

As he entered his suite in his flagship hotel in Athens, Nelios was struck by a new discovery. The room was cold. Not in temperature—no, the marble gleamed with sunlight and fresh lilies spilled fragrance from crystal vases—but cold in the way only a room teeming with bitterness and acrimony could be.

Thee mou, if he could sense this in the air, did he even want to know what was happening inside him? What Vayle saw each time she looked at him, took him into her body?

Agnes sat ramrod-straight on the edge of a silk-covered chaise, a cup of untouched tea in her hand. She wore her apprehension like a shroud, but she managed to summon a smile. 'Nelios. It's good to see you.'

He stood opposite her, back to the unlit fireplace, arms crossed, jaw tight.

Her keen gaze rested on him, searching. *For what?* he wanted to snap. Signs that he was broken, past the point of no return? He bit his tongue.

'You have a beautiful place,' she continued. 'It looks even better in reality than it did from the pictures.'

She was making conversation to cover the awkwardness. Against his will, something softened inside him. 'A tour will be arranged if you wish.'

Not by him, though. A handful of months ago, he would've jumped at the opportunity to further demonstrate how far he'd come without a single helping hand. But he'd only been away from Apeiron a matter of hours and he was already at breaking point.

The voice screaming inside that he'd made a mistake leaving Vayle and Angelos clamoured louder. What if she carried through with her threat to leave? Could he even blame her if she did?

'Maybe later, thank you.'

He imagined Vayle's wide, relieved smile at discovering he was here with Agnes and patted himself on the back. Brownie points with his wife were important.

Why, when it might not be enough to…to…?

His muscles tensed as the churning intensified. Damn it. The last time he'd walked a rope this tight was in that alley. But he'd come through that. He would come through this too. Put his past to bed, as Vayle had so passionately advocated. Maybe then he could finally seek greater pleasures.

Satisfied with that direction, he pinned his gaze on the woman who'd given him life then treated it so carelessly. And for a moment, he saw her—not the woman who'd disappeared from his life without a fight, but his mother. She was haunted and human. Flawed, as Vayle had insisted.

'You've been avoiding me.'

'I had practice,' he replied. 'You avoided me for half my childhood.'

Her breath hitched. 'I deserve that.'

He didn't deny it. He just let the silence stretch until it crackled.

'So,' he said, voice like glass, 'Let's get on with this. You've asked to see me often enough. Let's talk.'

She swallowed, nodded. 'Since the sin was mine, I guess I'll start?'

It should've appeased him that she was finally taking the blame, but all Nelios felt was a deepening of that hollow in his soul. It took several moments of prying open that rage-filled emptiness, forcing himself to look into the chasm to recognise what he felt. Fury, yes. Pain, definitely. But… sorrow too, for all the wasted years.

'Was it worth it?' he asked, his voice weary. Another question he'd buried deep, pulling it out only when the demons won and he couldn't fight the vault of pain.

Her mouth quivered. 'In hindsight? No.' Her voice was barely above a whisper. Then she shook her head. 'That's not quite true. This path I took, it brought me Vayle.'

His heart shredded. 'A fair trade, I suppose. How lucky for you to be able to toss one child away and pick up—'

'Stop saying that! I never tossed you away. We always planned to come back for you. At least, I did. Always.' Her voice brimmed with the kind of certainty that battered his fury.

'There were so many ways you could've ensured what happened to me didn't happen. Even at twelve, I could've told you that. And, you forget, I overheard everything you and Apostolis discussed. There was never a second, third or fourth option. You chose foster care, without doing your due diligence or even caring where I landed.'

He stopped, collected himself. 'I want to know why,' he said at last, low and controlled. The kind of quietness that masked years of rage. 'Why you left me. Why you, my mother, chose to trust a complete stranger with your son's wellbeing. Then you got on a plane and forgot all about him.'

Agnes flinched—actually flinched. 'It wasn't that simple.'

'No?' He stepped closer, gaze hard. 'Because from where I stood—alone, confused, in a stranger's care—it looked very simple.'

Her hands trembled around her tea cup. 'You were never supposed to stay in foster care. The woman was recommended by Apostolis's friend. He owned a care company.

And it was only meant to be temporary, just a few months, while things settled.'

He laughed then, sharp and humourless. '"While things settled". You mean until your pockets were fat enough? Did you even bother to call to check on me?'

'Yes. I called the foster carer once a week, every week.' Her face crumbled. 'I was told it was best not to speak to you myself and unsettle you, as you were already making friends…'

'Of course, you believed her. You wanted your conscience appeased.'

Her lips trembled and she didn't even need to confirm that. He saw it written all over her face.

'I thought you were happy, and the situation at the hotel was extremely challenging. I expect Vayle has told you about her father?'

'Another monster who shouldn't have been allowed to sire children.'

'*Parakaló*, don't say that,' she begged.

Aware his emotions were near to imploding, he reined himself in. Settling back, he stared at her. 'Fine. Go on, then.'

'I came back for you—six months later. When I realised I was being put off. Discouraged from asking questions.'

Shock rushed to fill the hollows inside him, then he shook his head. 'That's a lie! You never came back.'

She sent him a sad smile. 'I came, but no one knew what had happened to you. I eventually traced you to a home that had burned down.' She wept silently, shaking her head in despair. 'I was so terrified…' She stumbled to a stop.

Nelios was reeling from the revelation that she'd returned to find him herself. And from a niggling he couldn't quite pinpoint.

'So you came for me. And left again. Then what?'

'Every moment I could spare, I came back to Athens. But you…you seemed to have vanished off the face of the earth.'

His lips pursed. 'Between the authorities, who were very keen to lock me away in another home and throw away the key, and unsavoury characters who preyed on children my age, I was forced to become a master at hiding on the streets.'

She flinched. Her hand darted out, beseeching. He clenched his gut because his feelings were in danger of softening, her pain feeding into his. And he couldn't afford that.

Then the niggling congealed into a tangible question. 'You keep saying "I". Where was Apostolis?' he demanded.

Tears filled her eyes, and a different hollow opened inside him.

'Forgive me, Nelios. We… I was always going to tell you when you were older…'

'Tell me what?' His voice as sharp as a scalpel digging straight into his heart. Because that heart *knew* what was coming.

Her eyes closed. 'Apostolis was not your father.'

That stopped him, numbed him from head to heel.

'What?'

Agnes's hand twisted in her lap. 'You were conceived before I met him. I was young, naïve. Your biological father left before you were born. Apostolis had always wanted me and he married me to save my reputation. To give you a name.'

Nelios stared at her. The floor had shifted under him, but still he didn't move. 'And he hated me for it.'

'Not at first, but…' Her voice cracked. 'Eventually, he

resented how much I loved you. He saw you as a barrier to me loving him. And he...he gave me an ultimatum.'

He swallowed. 'Say it.'

'He said it was him or you.'

Silence.

Nelios stepped back as though she'd struck him. 'And you chose him,' he whispered.

'I thought I could fix his relationship with you. That if I kept the marriage intact, he would relent and I could bring you back. But time passed and—he made it impossible. Every time I tried, he reminded me of what I owed him. And I couldn't stand against him.'

'Yes,' he said, voice low and lethal. 'You were a coward.'

She didn't argue. 'Yes, I was.'

The truth settled between them, finally out in the open.

'You were my mother,' he said, softer now, but somehow more brutal. 'You were supposed to fight for me.'

'I know.' More tears slid down her cheek, catching the light like glass. 'And I'll never forgive myself. But you must know—I loved you, Nelios. I loved you so much. And that's why he came to hate you. Because you were always mine.

'A year—that was all I planned to be away from you, regardless of what Lancaster or Tolis wanted. Not...'

Two decades.

His throat burned and his fists clenched, but the dam didn't break. Not yet.

He turned away, facing the tall windows. The sun outside was too bright, too cruel. But he let it burn him.

'I don't know if I can forgive you,' he said after a long pause. 'Not yet.'

Agnes nodded. 'Then I'll wait. For as long as it takes.'

He didn't answer. Just stood there in the wreckage of

his life, knowing it was indeed too late. He had nothing to offer Vayle, after all.

Nothing at all.

Agnes continued to speak. 'I also hired a private detective to look for you.'

Another bolt of shock lanced his middle. 'You hired a detective?' he echoed woodenly.

'*Ne*. But that went nowhere.'

He knew why. He, Andreas and Capaldi had paid a fisherman to smuggle them into Sicily on his boat so they could find menial work on a vineyard. He'd scrimped and saved for the better part of two and a half years. He'd returned to Athens and bought his first hotel for pennies, courtesy of the failing economy. He'd put in the papers to change his name the same day and never looked back.

Her soft sobbing refocused his attention on her. 'The investigator said it was likely you were...' She stopped, unable to form the words.

He spoke them for her. 'You were led to believe I was dead.' And here, now, was the *exodus* he'd always wished for. But, rather than experience the satisfaction of a well-earned denouement, his own personal Greek tragedy appeared entirely formed of acts of poor judgement and mistimed endeavours.

'Until Vayle and I heard from your lawyer wanting her hotel.' She rose, approached and caught his hand in hers, gripping it tightly. 'Forgive me. *Parakalo*. There wasn't a single day when I didn't think about you. Regret what I did.'

Nelios didn't pull away.

But, even as he allowed himself to absorb the series of unfortunate circumstances that had brought him to this point, something whispered to him that he'd been irreparably altered.

In a way neither he nor anyone else might be able to fix.

Vayle opened the French doors and started walking, just as she'd done yesterday after putting Angelos down for his nap. Nelios had been gone just under twenty-four hours. It felt like years.

She walked past the middle point of the island, through the olive and orange groves, skirting the craggy beach and climbing the cliff till she reached the highest point. There she sat, watching the waves crash relentlessly against the rocks below. Salt spray mixed with tears she didn't want to dash away as an hour passed, maybe two.

It was good to get it all out so she could be strong for Angelos…for the new life she carried. With a hiccup, she slid her hand over her belly, heavier emotions clogging her throat. She hadn't even had time to absorb this miraculous news until now. Now she had, an untouched piece of her heart filled with love her for the baby growing inside her. 'I will love you too, through thick and thin. I promise you.'

'Vayle.'

She shook her head, believing the deep echo of her name was a trick of the wind.

'*Agapita*, please come away from the edge.'

Startled, she glanced over her shoulder in time to catch Nelios's deep flinch and paling face. She didn't want to hope and couldn't bear another bout of rejection, so she faced the turbulent view once more. 'Why should I?'

'Because watching you tumble off this cliff will be the tragic melodrama that finally kills me; I'm sure of it.'

She shrugged and kept facing forward. 'I'm feeling

melodramatic. I thought I'd come and see the literal expression of my feelings.'

'It would please me greatly if you stepped back a little more.'

Perhaps it was cruel to relish the strain in his voice. To know the thought of losing her shook *some* part of him. Anger bubbled up. She'd put everything on the line, and for what?

Her fingers tightened around the white plastic stick in her pocket, resenting the jolt of unjustified guilt she felt. She managed, *barely*, to kick herself out of that mindset. She'd done nothing wrong. They'd done this with their eyes wide open.

'I'm not in the mood to please you, Nelios. What are you doing here, anyway? Weren't you going to be in Athens for several days?'

'At the risk of more melodrama, I couldn't stay away.'

'It's a good thing then that this island is big enough. Until I leave, we can stay out of each other's way.'

A rough sound escaped him. 'So you're leaving?'

Misery filled her but she forced a nod. 'I don't see that I have a choice,' she said. Then waited…and waited.

When the tiny seeds of hope died, she snatched the plastic stick from her pocket. 'I don't know what you're doing back here so soon when you seemed hellbent on leaving, but I've already kept this from you when I should've told you yesterday.' She held the pregnancy test out to him.

For endless seconds he looked poleaxed. Then he lunged forward and snatched it from her, staring at it before his eyes met hers, then dropped to her belly. 'You're…'

'Pregnant with our second child? Yes. As fate would have it.'

His gaze dropped back to the test and this time she read

his emotions accurately: shock; pride; *elation*. But those emotions were locked away far too quickly, leaving behind a landscape that grew increasingly grey...inhospitable.

'I will be a good father to this child too, you have my word. But...' He paused, his chest heaving far too dramatically, rivalling the heaving in her soul. The certain knowledge he was about to knock her world to smithereens. 'I'm terrified that's all I can give, Vayle. After what I discovered...' He stopped, inhaled, then blew out his breath. 'If you're open to a fifty-fifty custody arrangement, I'll be in your debt for ever.'

Her heart squeezed, but she shook her head to clear it. 'What do you mean, what you discovered?'

A wave of guilt swept over his face. 'I met with Ag... my mother. She told me...' He shook his head. 'Forgive me for not listening to you, Vayle.'

'Not until you tell me everything. I have a right to know, I think.'

'Ne,' he agreed.

She listened as he retold his conversation with the woman who'd birthed him. Relief shuddered through her, over and over. Her every hope for him, for the woman she'd believed in who'd been like a mother to her, had been realised.

'So they came looking for you. They didn't abandon you,' she affirmed softly.

'*She* didn't, no.'

His emphasis made her stiffen. But she still couldn't bring herself to look at him. She waited, because there was more.

'Tolis wasn't my father.'

Her head snapped up. 'What?'

'I think, deep down, I always knew. We were never close.

And when he died the only regret I felt was never getting the chance to tell him what a poor parent he was.'

As he finished his story, her heart bled for him for a minute. Before she reined it in. Because she had a baby, *two* babies, to think of. And heartache to manage.

'Vayle, I feel… I can't… You did this for me. All of it. And I've been nothing but monstrous to you. How can I ever make it up to you?'

Nelios ventured closer, his every sinew straining to grab her, to anchor her to him, to snatch her back from the terrifying edge of loss. But he didn't. Couldn't—not yet. Instead, he crouched lower than her, heart in his throat, remorse bleeding from every pore. He'd spent so long protecting his pride, his pain, that he'd forgotten how to reach for what truly mattered. Only then might he avert the very exodus he'd foolishly claimed to crave—on his knees. Perhaps he deserved no less.

The weight of the small plastic stick still in his hand felt almost too sacred for his touch. A miracle, another undeserved gift from the woman whose love he'd abused with silence and distance. His fingers curled around it like a lifeline.

She didn't look at him. Her spine was stiff, her body drawn tight with grief she hadn't allowed to show until now. 'Take a tranquiliser,' she said, her voice sharp. 'Go lie down. You'll feel like yourself in no time, I'm sure.'

His lips twisted into a ghost of a smile, one that didn't feel as monstrous. That she could throw such cutting remarks even now… She was glorious. Far more than he'd ever had the right to dream of. But the smile died quickly. The agony of being parted from her returned to crush his chest like a vice.

'Drugs won't help, I fear,' he said, voice rough. 'Only gaining back the very thing I've spent my life throwing away might save me.'

She didn't move. But he saw it—the small hitch in her breath. The tiniest tremble in her fingers.

It was enough to let the floodgates open. 'You were right, *agapi mou*. About everything.' His voice cracked. 'I was a coward. I've been running all my life. Hiding behind righteousness and pain because it made it easier to believe I didn't need love. That I didn't *deserve* love.'

He shook his head, shame slicing through his soul. 'Watching you give it so freely, so wholeheartedly… I made myself believe it was weakness to want you. That what you were offering couldn't possibly be real. So, yes, I fought it—you, us. I fought the very thing I now know was my salvation.'

Still no response. But he didn't stop. He couldn't.

'I convinced myself I was incapable of love. That I was too damaged, broken. That I'd been discarded once, so I should protect myself.' He swallowed. 'It was easier than facing the truth—that loving you scared me more than anything in this world.'

She turned then, slowly. Her eyes were fire, storm and heartbreak. 'You're not broken,' she said, her voice sharp with pain. 'Stop saying that. Stop *believing* that.'

His heart crumpled at the raw conviction in her words. 'Maybe I'm not, not any more, because you saw something in me when I saw nothing. Because you gave. And gave. I witnessed a warm, generous, loving woman who would go to the ends of the earth for the lucky ones who called her theirs. And I—I rejected you, every time, like a fool.'

'So you came to tell me you've seen the light. Now what?'

He edged closer, pulse thundering in his ears and true terror gripping his insides. Because that agony he heard in her voice—he'd caused it.

'I came back thinking I'd lost you. That I'd finally succeeded in destroying the only good thing in my life. And the truth is—I don't want to live without you, Vayle. I can't. I couldn't even breathe on that plane on the way home. It felt like I was being flayed open, cell by cell.'

A sound escaped her—choked, disbelieving.

He pressed a fist to his chest. 'This? This pain? I recognise it now. It's love. It's *you*. And, if you give me a second chance, I swear I'll spend the rest of my life earning every breath you give me. Every smile. Every piece of your trust I've shattered.'

He dared to touch her—just a fingertip to her wrist. She didn't pull away. She said nothing for an eternity. But her eyes...*thee mou*, her breathtaking eyes created his every vision of heaven.

'I should make you wait. Make you suffer. But I just don't have it in me, *agapu*,' she murmured.

His heart tumbled over. He ventured another inch closer and touched her back. Felt her sway towards him. '*S'agapo*, Vayle. You are my air, my gravity, my home. Forgive me. I'm a fool for waiting this long to grasp the gift you were giving me. I love you. Please forgive me.'

For a moment, the sky itself seemed to hold its breath. Then, with a soft, broken cry, she twisted and launched herself into his arms. He caught her like a drowning man clutching his final hope, this treasure he'd come so close to losing. She fitted against him as she always had—effortlessly, like destiny.

'I love you too, Nelios!'

His heart soared, so high and free he wondered if his

feet would ever touch the ground. God, he hoped not. He held her tighter and crushed her close, his own tears hot against her skin.

'Thank you. Thank you for still having space in your heart for me.'

She pulled back just far enough to cup his face. 'It was always yours, even when it hurt. Even when you walked away.'

'My love, can I coax you away from the edge now, please?' he breathed reverently, trembling. 'My heart really can't take it and I very much need to kiss you.'

Her laugh was husky and tear-tinged as she nodded.

He stood and scooped her into his arms, cradling her tenderly. Slowly, carefully, he brought her away from the cliff, from the precipice of everything they'd nearly lost.

Then, right there beneath the sky, in his favourite place on earth, and in the arms of the purest love he didn't deserve but fully intended to keep, he kissed Vayle. It was long, slow and deep until every chasm filled and overflowed.

She was flushed and her eyes glittered beautifully when he lifted his head. 'Can we go home now? We have a contract to rip up and forever to plan, I believe.'

He brushed his thumb over her cheek. 'We do. I should never have left you, my heart, even for a day. Now I'm back, I'll spend every moment proving I'm worthy of you.'

When she burrowed into his neck, Nelios held her tighter.

He wasn't falling any more. He was home.

EPILOGUE

Sofia Agnes Petralis was born at home on Apeiron to a mildly terrified father who then broke into reams of smiles, showering kisses the second he held his daughter.

And for the next three nights he straight refused to leave the nursery, completely in love and in awe as he experienced every small gesture his baby girl made.

Vayle had yearned to see what a besotted Nelios would look like in those testing weeks before they'd confessed their love. Now it was almost overwhelming.

Not that she took it for granted. They'd been through fire and anguish to get to where they were today. Seeing Nelios and Agnes finally at peace with one another was heart-warming. *Healing*.

'It's time, *agapita*.'

She turned at the low, sexy rumble and smiled when Nelios strode towards her. Her heart flipped at the sight of their daughter cradled in his big hands, the bib thrown over his shoulder as he carefully propped Sofia up and held out his hand to Vayle.

Slotting the hoop into her ear, she checked that her cream-and-yellow sundress was in place and crossed the room.

'I'm ready. Guess I can't be fashionably late to my own baby's christening, huh?'

He smiled, his heated eyes trailing appreciatively over her body before lingering on her mouth. 'We have time for me to steal a kiss then, *ne*, we must go. Andreas is vocalising his unhappiness at being kept waiting to hold his god-daughter. Capaldi is aiding that rebellion.'

She rolled her eyes but smiled.

She'd agreed wholeheartedly when Nelios had asked his two trusted friends to be godfathers to their children. Now that she knew what they'd been through, she was certain both men would move heaven and earth to protect them if needed.

Nelios caught her in a one-armed hold, pulled her close and sealed his mouth onto hers, kissing her until they had to come up for air. His forehead touched hers and they breathed each other in, just for another moment. 'My heart is full. You've made me so happy, *eros mou*. I love you, so much.'

Vayle blinked back tears, reaching up to wipe the traces of lipstick from his mouth. 'If it's half as much as I love you, then I'm so glad I stowed away on your plane.'

He laughed as he caught her hand and led her out of their bedroom. 'Indeed. And I'm thrilled I let you.'

As his senses compelled him to do these days, Nelios sought out his son as soon as they stepped onto the terrace.

Angelos, now a boisterous sixteen-month-old, could barely sit still on his grandmother's knee. It became an impossibility the second he spotted his parents and sister. He bolted towards them, and his wife caught him up and perched him on her hips.

Nelios, attempting to look stern but failing, walked with his family to the aisle of the tiny chapel, then tried to keep himself together as his daughter was baptised.

And failed. Not a single soul dared to call him on it, though. So he presumed some of his monstrous reputation remained unsullied.

Later, he was celebrating his many bounties when his friends joined him beneath the largest orange tree in his grove as the sun went down. For a moment, all three men observed the festivities, Vayle charming their guests and spreading her infectious joy all around.

'Never thought I'd see the day,' Andreas muttered after swallowing a mouthful of beer.

'Me neither,' Capaldi agreed.

Nelios shrugged. 'What can I say? I'm a changed man and it feels fucking great.'

They slapped his shoulder, laughed and drank some more.

Until a ping from Andreas's phone distracted his friend. Nelios's eyes narrowed at Andreas's dark expression. 'Everything okay?'

'It will be. But I need to go.'

'To Athens or Sicily?' he asked, hoping it wasn't the latter—for his friend's sake and the family ties to the mafia Andreas had been trying to escape all his life—but fearing it was.

His jaw clenched. 'Sicily.'

It was Nelios's turn to slap his friend's shoulder. 'Go, my friend. But if you need me, I'll be there.'

'Me too,' Capaldi echoed.

They watched him leave, then Capaldi was distracted by his wife and kids.

And, even before he walked away, Nelios strode towards his own, a compulsion he fully surrendered to drawing him to the love of his life.

'Everything okay?' Vayle murmured, sliding her arms around him.

Nelios watched his wife kiss his daughter then hug their son, pure adoration on her face.

He wrapped his arms around his wife and kissed her. Then dropped his forehead to hers.

'With you here in my arms and an abundance of love around me? Absolutely.'

* * * * *

Were you captivated by Keeping a Greek Secret*? Then why not explore these other steamy stories from Maya Blake?*

Greek Pregnancy Clause
Enemy's Game of Revenge
Crowned for His Son
Out of Office Nights
Snowbound and Royally Forbidden

Available now!

Get up to 4 Free Books!

We'll send you 2 free books from each series you try PLUS a free Mystery Gift.

FREE Value Over **$25**

Both the **Harlequin Presents** and **Harlequin Medical Romance** series feature exciting stories of passion and drama.

YES! Please send me 2 FREE novels from Harlequin Presents or Harlequin Medical Romance and my FREE gift (gift is worth about $10 retail). After receiving them, if I don't wish to receive any more books, I can return the shipping statement marked "cancel." If I don't cancel, I will receive 6 brand-new larger-print novels every month and be billed just $7.19 each in the U.S., or $7.99 each in Canada, or 4 brand-new Harlequin Medical Romance Larger-Print books every month and be billed just $7.19 each in the U.S. or $7.99 each in Canada, a savings of 20% off the cover price. It's quite a bargain! Shipping and handling is just 50¢ per book in the U.S. and $1.25 per book in Canada.* I understand that accepting the 2 free books and gift places me under no obligation to buy anything. I can always return a shipment and cancel at any time. The free books and gift are mine to keep no matter what I decide.

Choose one:
☐ **Harlequin Presents Larger-Print** (176/376 BPA G36Y)
☐ **Harlequin Medical Romance** (171/371 BPA G36Y)
☐ **Or Try Both!** (176/376 & 171/371 BPA G36Z)

Name (please print)

Address   Apt. #

City   State/Province   Zip/Postal Code

Email: Please check this box ☐ if you would like to receive newsletters and promotional emails from Harlequin Enterprises ULC and its affiliates. You can unsubscribe anytime.

> Mail to the **Harlequin Reader Service:**
> **IN U.S.A.:** P.O. Box 1341, Buffalo, NY 14240-8531
> **IN CANADA:** P.O. Box 603, Fort Erie, Ontario L2A 5X3

Want to explore our other series or interested in ebooks? Visit www.ReaderService.com or call 1-800-873-8635.

---

*Terms and prices subject to change without notice. Prices do not include sales taxes, which will be charged (if applicable) based on your state or country of residence. Canadian residents will be charged applicable taxes. Offer not valid in Quebec. This offer is limited to one order per household. Books received may not be as shown. Not valid for current subscribers to the Harlequin Presents or Harlequin Medical Romance series. All orders subject to approval. Credit or debit balances in a customer's account(s) may be offset by any other outstanding balance owed by or to the customer. Please allow 4 to 6 weeks for delivery. Offer available while quantities last.

Your Privacy—Your information is being collected by Harlequin Enterprises ULC, operating as Harlequin Reader Service. For a complete summary of the information we collect, how we use this information and to whom it is disclosed, please visit our privacy notice located at https://corporate.harlequin.com/privacy-notice. Notice to California Residents – Under California law, you have specific rights to control and access your data. For more information on these rights and how to exercise them, visit https://corporate.harlequin.com/california-privacy. For additional information for residents of other U.S. states that provide their residents with certain rights with respect to personal data, visit https://corporate.harlequin.com/other-state-residents-privacy-rights/.